P9-DEP-419

# Apartment 1986

Also by Lisa Papademetriou:

*A Tale of Highly Unusual Magic*

# Apartment 1986

by Lisa Papademetriou

HARPER

*An Imprint of* HarperCollins*Publishers*

Apartment 1986

 For information address HarperCollins Children's Books, a division of HarperCollins Publishers, 195 Broadway, New York, NY 10007.
www.harpercollinschildrens.com

Library of Congress Control Number: 2016940571
ISBN 978-0-06-237108-9

Typography by Sarah Creech
17 18 19 20 21 PC/LSCH 10 9 8 7 6 5 4 3 2 1

First Edition

*For everyone who is smarter than they sound*

*and deeper than they look.*

## CHAPTER ONE

# In which the heroine (me!) practices the power of positive thinking

I AM BEGINNING TO think that maybe I will be a philosopher when I grow up. That is what my mother always says, "Our Callie is such a philosopher," and I am really beginning to believe her. I am always having important thoughts all of the time, and let me tell you, they can be Very Deep. Sometimes, they are so deep that I barely understand them! Like this one: a journey of a thousand miles may begin with a single step, but it also ends with one.

I mean—BOOM! I just blew your mind, right? I know it doesn't exactly make sense yet, but I think if I keep working on it, I can at least put it on a mug.

Because that is the problem with philosophizing—my father says that it does not pay very well, and I think we all know that it is very hard to make a living these days. That is why I have decided that *my* kind of philosophy is the kind that will make money. I will become what's known as a *guru*, like Althea Orris.

Althea has a mega–bestselling book, a late-night show on the Positivity Power Network, and a YouTube channel. I love her because her philosophy is based on both positive thinking and economics. She believes in the law of inertia and in gravity and in quantum mechanics, but *also* the basic idea is that if you think happy thoughts, you can make happy things happen. If you have sad thoughts, sad things happen. And Althea herself is the proof of this, because she thought happy things and now she is a bestselling author and guru. That is why it is so important to think happy thoughts *as much as possible*. If you start to feel sad, you must SNAP OUT OF IT. RIGHT AWAY! Because bad thoughts are like poison.

Althea's personal motto is: Keep It Happy! She sells all kinds of T-shirts and water bottles that say Keep It Happy! on them, and that is another thing that has made her superrich. I want my philosophy to be like that.

Right now, I am trying to have totally positive thoughts

about the fact that I am about to spend ninety minutes in detention. It's held in the library and we are allowed to do our homework, so it is actually quite educational and convenient. (Positive!) The Haverton library is small, but it is a very nice place and there are a lot of plants in it and a few comfortable chairs, which makes the whole place seem very homelike. (Positive!) It is my second-favorite place in the school, so that is also positive. (Positive!)

Ms. Thumb is in charge of detention because she is the librarian and detention is part of her job. I like her because she always knows what I should read and she understands that a girl likes drama when it's romantic, but maybe not so much when it's all about depressed people and their parents dying and whatnot. In my opinion, books and art should be mostly happy because of Keep It Happy!

When Ms. Thumb sees me, she just says, "Hello, Callie," kind of like she's glad to see me but knows that she should not be because I am in detention. She is young, for a librarian, because everyone knows that librarians are supposed to be older than gravel, and I know that Ms. Thumb is special because she is pretty and knows about Twitter and stuff, even though my friend Min says nobody uses that anymore, and everyone is on PicBomb.

We interrupt this fascinating bulletin to announce that a Special Guest Star has just walked in through the door!

I lift my eyebrows at Zelda Waverly, my best new friend, who just shakes her head and slips into a chair. Sometimes, I even wonder if I am telepathological, because between our two looks, I swear, we have just had this conversation:

Me: *What are you doing in here? You never have detention!*

Zelda: *I can't even. My mom is going to kill me if she finds out!*

She puts her forehead down and her blond hair spills across the glossy oak in a very tragic cascade. I try not to feel envious that Zelda manages to look beautiful and compelling even when overdramatically serving a detention in the school library. (Hmm . . . jealousy is negative. Fix that!)

So I take out my book and start working on my math problems, which are supereasy because we are studying fractions and my teacher, Mr. Ziller, is excellent at explaining math things, unlike Ms. Way at my old school. She never used to let us ask questions because she said that if we asked questions she would never get through the lesson. But Mr. Ziller gets really happy if you ask a question, like you have absolutely made his day and he sometimes gets so excited to explain the answer that he has to breathe slowly into his fists for a minute to calm down. Of course, Ms. Way had thirty-four students in a class and Mr. Ziller only has eight, so maybe his job is easier. It's hard to tell.

My old school is in an "underserved community" in Jersey City, and my new school is in what I guess you would call an "overserved community" called the Upper East Side of New York City. We moved here over the summer because my dad got a new job as an accountant for some financial firm where they were paying him basically more money than God's deejay, and we got this really fancy apartment, and I got accepted to this really fancy school, and everything was completely too good to be true until somebody must have had a *really* bad thought, because the firm collapsed three weeks ago.

I have been trying to help my dad stay positive, though. It's like I always say, "Whenever God closes a door, he opens a window, so you can totally still climb out as long as you are on the first floor."

Think about it.

Ms. Thumb comes and stands beside my table. "This is the big one. You know that, right?"

I nod. I have a lot of tardy slips. Three tardy slips equals a detention. This is my third detention, because of nine tardies, and from here on out things escalate quickly. One more, and it's Principal Conference time. Like my parents aren't both having mental breakdowns *already*.

I am not in detention because I am a bad kid and break a lot of rules. I am a good kid and I only break one rule, which is that I like to go up to the roof of the school and look at the sky during lunch sometimes. Look, there are moments when a girl just needs a breath of air, and you can't get it inside this stuffy school or anywhere in Manhattan when you are down on the street. The air down there isn't air, it's basically 80 percent exhaust fumes and 25 percent heat and 25 percent dirt, which most of the time gets caught in your lip gloss which is *ew*. So if you want to breathe and maybe look at a few clouds, you have to get someplace up high. This is part of my philosophy: you can't have your head in the clouds unless your feet are firmly on the roof.

If you ask me, it shouldn't even be against the rules to go and get a breath of fresh air, but it is because technically the door to the roof is supposed to be locked but sometimes it isn't locked and by that I mean that it's always a smart idea to be nice to Selena who is on the janitorial crew because she might just have an extra key to the roof as long as I don't tell anyone where I got it.

Selena is the only person in authority at this school who understands that a girl sometimes needs to take a breath.

Anyway, the technical *technical* truth is that I am not really in trouble for being on the roof because nobody knows that I was on the roof. I am in trouble for being *late to class*, which happens sometimes *because I cannot hear the bell ring* while I am on the roof.

So.

"Don't blow it," Ms. Thumb says, and I give her this nod that means, "I hopefully won't."

I spend the rest of my detention doing social studies and then finally Ms. Thumb says that we can go. I walk over to Zelda and ask, "What's up?"

"Uniform infraction," she says. She sounds totally miserable. "Ms. Blount got me. She screamed at me in the hallway after lunch."

I make a sympathetic noise because I understand that

it is very difficult to think positive thoughts when one is being yelled at.

"I'm going to be in so much trouble." Zelda shoves her little purple notebook into her bag. "I was supposed to have a meeting with Janice this afternoon."

"Oooooooh." Janice is this world-famous private college guidance counselor. Yes, Zelda has a college guidance counselor, even though we are in the seventh grade. She meets with her once a month so that they can analyze "gaps" in Zelda's "experience and progress" and "seize opportunities for personal growth" when they "arise." My mom tried to get me to see Janice, but she has a seven-year waiting list, so I will hopefully be in college or at least far away by the time she is available.

"My mom has already texted me twenty times." Zelda looks at her phone like she is afraid of it. "What am I going to tell her?" Zelda asks.

I do not know what to say to this. "Um, could you tell her that you were doing extracurricular work helping orphaned dolphins, or something educational and extra-credity?"

Zelda laughs. "Callie, you're so hilarious."

That's hilarious? Because that's what I told *my* mother all the other times I was in detention. Mom was born in Ohio, and she is so confused by my new school that she pretty much believes anything I say about it. Like, if I told her they served space rocks for lunch, she would probably be like, "Wow, were they *crunchy*?" Because my mother is convinced that Haverton is chock-full of first-rate learning opportunities that you simply cannot have at a public institution, or whatever it says on the brochure.

Zelda sighs and texts her mom back, and then we both walk down three flights of stairs and out the front doors together. She lives a block uptown from the school, and I live five blocks downtown, but before we walk off in opposite directions, she says, "So—you're coming Friday, right?"

"Right," I say. "Of course."

"Because Mom is kind of bugging me. I hate to be—"

"No, no . . . I'll get you the check! Sorry; I just forgot." Ugggh. My stomach is swimming in stress acid. *Why did I ever say I would go to this thing?* The tickets are *two hundred and fifty dollars*, and Zelda's mom already bought one for me, *oh my god.*

I'm sure Dad has forgotten all about this plan, which he agreed to almost two months ago, back when he still had a job. I don't even know how to bring it up anymore. How can I ask him for two hundred and fifty dollars? I am being perfectly serious when I say that I would rather ask him for a kidney right now.

I don't even like Lucas Zev, but all the other girls think he's basically a musical genius and also really hot, even though his hair looks like it got stuck in a Roomba. But I was like *whatever I'll go* because my dad has been bugging me to get to know Zelda ever since he found out that her father is president of a giant music company business conglobberate thing.

"Text me later," Zelda says.

"Okay," I say, but then I am afraid that she will ask me about Lucas Zev if I text her later, so I add, "But I might be at a party thing tonight."

"What party?" Zelda asks. Because, let's face it, nobody throws a party at our school without inviting Zelda.

"Uh, it's a fund-raiser . . . for . . ." I look around for inspiration and see a woman walking a dog in a small plaid coat. "Chihuahua awareness." OMG, what? Thanks, mouth!

"Oh, that's great," Zelda says. "That region has so many challenges right now."

And that makes me happy, because: a) I did not even know that Chihuahua was a region, but apparently it is and now what I just said made sense, and b) it is nice to have smart friends.

Zelda blows me a kiss, and I feel a bit guilty for lying to her and about the whole ticket situation. I turn to go and find I am thinking about people who just disappear, you know, vanish without a trace, and I wonder if I could do that. You know you are stressed out when you are looking around Madison Avenue and kind of maybe hoping that you will fall down an open manhole and disappear in some very Manhattanesque way and then everyone could just *forget* about the money you owe them and just feel sort of sad and solemn when they think about you until they stop thinking about you (and the money) at all.

But this is not positive! So I tell myself to snap out of it.

*Okay, just think: how would Althea handle this?*

That's easy. She would say that if you truly believe that the money will appear, then it will. This is one of my favorite inspirational quotes: Positive Power is about being *positive* that what you want is right around the corner!

So I begin to concentrate on making two hundred and fifty dollars appear. First, I visualize a bunch of one-dollar bills, but then I realize it is easier to visualize two one-hundred-dollar bills and a fifty, and then I decide the easiest thing is to just picture three one-hundred-dollar bills, so I have enough money to get a concert T-shirt and everything—so that's what I do.

As I walk along, I think maybe I will find those crisp bills on the sidewalk. Like, maybe some really rich person dropped a big wad of cash when they stepped out of their limo! This is a very cheerful idea, and the longer I walk, the more certain I am that the money is out there, just waiting for me to find it!

And then, JUST AT THAT MOMENT, I spot a flash of green. It's—it is! It's money! It's a FIFTY-DOLLAR BILL!

I pick it up thinking, *Althea, thank you!* And then I see that my fifty-dollar bill is smaller than normal, and instead of an old president, there's a picture of a naked lady on it and *ew*, I realize this is just a flyer for a "gentlemen's club" and *ew* it was on the ground and EW, I touched it and I'M STILL TOUCHING IT! *EW*!

And so I let it go and it flutters away down the street and lands beside a fire hydrant.

Hm. That wasn't exactly a success . . .

. . . but I am pretty sure it was close!

I walk over to Fifth Avenue, where the food carts—coffee, gyros, pretzels, ice cream—are all lined up. I've got one earbud in, so the jumble of Manhattan noise blends with "Change of Heart" by Cyndi Lauper (I like old-school music), which works pretty well together. The sun is warm, so I decide that I have earned a smoothie and I stop at a new-looking cart with a giant pineapple painted on the side. And I am staring and staring at the list of smoothies, all of which have supercute names: Kale to the Chief, Strawberry the Hatchet, Singin' the Blues-berry, and I start to think about my old best friend, Anna, because her dad owns a food truck and makes the best enchiladas on earth, and I really wish that I could have one of those right now instead of some dumb kale drink.

And then I feel kind of sad, because Anna was, like, my best friend for eight years, and now I haven't spoken to her in months. Well, technically, she hasn't spoken to *me*. But that is another story that I am having Not One Drop of.

I order an Acai You Later smoothie and while I am waiting for it to blend, I hit Anna's number. She doesn't pick up, of course, so I leave a voice mail. "Hey, Anna! Hope you're good. I'm just thinking of you because I'm getting a smoothie and, uh, I hope you're good. Well, maybe we can talk sometime. Call me. Hope you're good. Bye."

Uggh. That voice mail was not my best work. I wish there were someone else I could call—someone who would answer the phone—but there really isn't.

Even though I like Zelda and my other best new friend, Min, I've only known them for eight months. And there is a big difference between a friend you have had for eight months and a friend you have had for eight years, even if you haven't spoken to the Eight-Year Friend for a while.

Okay, a long while.

I look up at the sky to make myself feel better, but sometimes the clouds are just too far away to help.

## CHAPTER TWO

# In which I make a momentulous decision

When I leave the apartment on Monday morning, I do *not* slam the door. That is because I do not believe in drama before 10 a.m. But also, I do not say good-bye to my parents. Because do you know what happened when I reminded them about the ticket to the Lucas Zev concert? They got into a fight.

This was the scene:

Dad: "She obviously can't go *now*, Helen."

Mom: "It's a networking opportunity! You never know what doors it could open—think about who Zelda's father is." Because this is how my dad got his last job: he went back to school to get a master's in business at Columbia University, and he networked like crazy. And that is how we went from being kinda regular middle class to being whatever we are now. "Besides, George, she already said she would."

Me: "Um, you guys? The ticket is, like, two hundred and fifty dollars? Just, you know, for your infor—"

Dad (horrified): "Helen, we can't just waste money now—she can sell the ticket on eBay!"

Me: "But then my friends would have to sit with some eBay weirdo?"

Mom: "You have to seize every unexpected opportunity!" I happen to know that this is the title of the latest business book my mom read to help her run her new fancy soap business, Scent With A Kiss. This is the business she started after she decided that being a social worker was too depressing.

Dad: "Are you kidding me? I have to talk to a lawyer at nine a.m.! Callie, you're not going."

Me: "What should I tell my friends?"

Dad: "Don't tell them anything; it's none of their business."

Uggggh. So I left.

I *did* give Desmond a little kiss on the head right before I ducked out, though. He didn't notice—he was watching some cartoon show about a purple blob that might or might not have been a plastic bag. I swear, kids' shows these days are so weird. Back when I was a kid, there was SpongeBob. I guess there is still SpongeBob, only it seems weird to me now. Anyway, Desmond was oblivious to all of the shouting, which is just as well.

Ray is at the door when I get off the elevator and I smile and say, "Hi, Ray," because I think it's always a good idea to be nice to the doorman. Because if you aren't nice to the doorman, they can send your packages to the wrong apartment, or give the Chinese food deliveryman a hard time and not let them in when you really need the food right away, like before *Project Runway* starts. Althea says that this is called karma, and if there is one thing I have learned from my grandmother's 1980s music, it's that karma is like a chameleon, which means it is *adorable.*

Anyway, Ray smiles at me and tips his hat, which I think is supercute and old-fashioned. One thing that Ray and I have in common is that we both have to wear a uniform, only his has this jaunty little hat and Haverton K–12 School for Girls does not allow hats in classrooms. Because of gangs. Which is a shame, because I look totally amazing in hats. I could totally see myself as a yacht captain someday.

Anyway, I head up Madison peeking in the shop windows. They are perfect for checking my full-body reflection. I adjust my sunglasses so that they are halfway down my nose (to make it look normal and not like my granddad's nostril-fest—thanks for the genes, Grandpa!), yank down my shirt, and then flouf it up again so that it looks casual. Then I give up. I never quite manage Zelda's look—like she just rolled out of bed looking rumpled yet perfect, which is probably what she did. She never has, like, a zit on her face or whatnot. Our other good friend, Min, is the same way. It's very aggregating.

I keep checking my reflection in the windows, so I end up basically scuttling sideways up the street. Like a lemur, or like those crazy running people in Central Park who are always jogging backward or sideways or carrying a tractor tire or whatnot because regular jogging is simply not challenging enough.

This makes me think that checking my reflection in the windows is kind of sort of an exercise, which cheers me up a little. Then my phone buzzes. It's a text from Zelda.

U coming to Lucas Zevvvv? Mom freaking; needs final head count.

Then there's an emoji that I don't really recognize—is it a battery with a smiley face? Uggh. My phone is actually my mom's old smartphone, and I'm still kind of bad at using it.

*Yes,* I type in, even though I'm not really sure. Zelda's mom is beautiful and terrifying. I super don't want her mad at me. I managed to put this off for a whole weekend, but now I can't avoid it. *Sorry. Eep.*

Zelda: NBD. She's driving me crazy.

Me: But doesn't that make her happy?

Zelda: Lolz, Callie, you're h'lair.

I stand there wondering how to respond to that text because I wasn't really trying to be funny but then three little dots appear, like fingers tapping on a tabletop, which tells me that Zelda is typing again. Finally, the text pops up: *We are gonna have a blasssssstttt!!!* Followed by twenty emojis: a party hat, a horn, a camel (?), a smiley face, a winky face, streamers, a cruise ship, a tree, and something that looks like a hockey stick. No clue.

I send a smiley face back. Emojis are not really where I shine. Like, there was one that I thought was chocolate ice cream for the longest time, so I would send it whenever something was yum and people were like *ew* and then I realized it was not chocolate ice cream, after all. I wish emojis came with little explanations about what they *mean*—like, "I'm feeling happy!" Or, "Life is like this penguin!"—it would be so helpful.

The clock on my phone says 7:21. I was so eager to get out of the apartment this morning that I'm going to be crazy early for school, and I suddenly realize that I have time to drop by Grandma Hildy's apartment. That makes me happy, because I can maybe get inspired and shake off these yucky money worries. And then I think of a cool thought that might even be good on a T-shirt someday: always look on the bright side, because it is totally hard to see in the dark.

Lots of people could use that one!

Grandma Hildy lives really close to Haverton, and I drop in on her a lot. Usually *after* school, but she gets up at six, so it's not like I'll be waking her. I detour down Eighty-Eighth Street.

Robert, my grandma's doorman, is hosing down the sidewalk under the long green awning. He frowns at me as I give him a wave. When I reach the nineteenth floor, I notice that something is sticking out of the plant that my grandmother has placed in the little nook by her front door. It's a small plastic box. When I pick it up, I see that someone has written down a list of titles, and I realize what this is—it is a cassette. I think that is cute, because my grandmother likes antiques. The song titles also sound pretty good: "What Is Love?," "Just Like Heaven," "Love Is a Stranger," "Love My Way." I know the song "Do You Really Want to Hurt Me?" It's by Culture Club. I love Culture Club, but not as much as I love Cyndi Lauper.

I slide the tape back into the plant. I have no idea why my grandmother would have put it there, but I don't dare to question it. Grandma Hildy likes stuff how she likes it, and that's it.

I poke the doorbell under the brass number 2086 and then walk right in. My grandmother never locks her front door. She says Robert is the best security. Most people basically have to give him a DNA test to get in.

"Grandma?" I call. "Gran?"

The apartment is still. A tablet computer sits on the sage green couch, but the screen is dark. Beyond the window, this strange fog hangs over the city, like a . . . well, *not* like a blanket. Blankets are thin. I can't see the sky at all, so this is more like a comforter, I guess. It's pretty, but I can usually see all the way to the Met from Grandma's window, and now I can't see anything, not even the street. It's like I am in a cloud, and I imagine this apartment floating in the air with nothing below and only sky above.

"Gran?" I call again, walking into the narrow kitchen.

A sweet scent hangs in the air. It's like vanilla and orange and something else. A small plate and her favorite coffee mug—World's Greatest Grandma!, courtesy of guess who—are in the sink. Probably Sherlock Holmes could do something with all of this information, but all I know is that my grandmother isn't here.

I'm surprised at the hollow feeling in my chest and the heaviness in my arms. I hadn't realized how much I wanted to talk to my grandmother this morning.

There's a movement from the dark hall, and Biddy walks in, eyes her food dish, and looks up at me as if she thinks I'm going to do something about it. She gives me her usual meow, which sounds like a motor that can't quite make up its mind to start: *Me-uh-uh-uh-uh?*

"Girlfriend, you know you're on a diet. Sorry."

Her green eyes give me this look, like, *If this is all I can eat, why live?* And, honestly, her gray fur is so fluffy and she looks really good carrying a little extra padding, and what's one treat in the scheme of things, and who wants a skinny cat, and lots of other things run through my head, so I go to the jar and say, "Okay, but just one," and I give her a treat. She takes it so happily that I give her another. Then one more, and I shut the lid. "It's called *restraint*," I tell her as she winds through my legs.

My phone buzzes again. It's Min.

*What r u weering on fiday?????????* Min has fat thumbs, and is the world's worst texter. My hand starts to vibrate—now Min is calling.

"Hello?"

"Did you get my text?"

"The one you sent one second ago?"

"Okay, you got it! What are you wearing on Friday?"

"I don't know, maybe—"

"Oh, Lord, Callie, you're hopeless. I hope you're wearing the white dress."

"The white—?"

"With the gold shoes."

Gold shoes?

"The ones you wore at Beyoncé's party?" Min prompts me.

Oh, right! I *do* have gold shoes. I only ever wore them once, though, and that was to a wedding six months ago. Although, uh, I might have told Min something about a party on a yacht. It's like Althea says: "Sometimes there is a very fine line between reality and wishful thinking."

"So here is my question—" Min goes on. "What should *I* wear?"

"Why don't you ask your mom?"

"Because she buys everything at L.L. Bean." Min's mom is a pediatric heart surgeon—she wears a lot of scrubs and things that look like scrubs. "Should I wear the new jumpsuit, or the tank dress?"

"Have I seen either one of those?"

"I'll send you some selfies and you can text me back. Okay? See you in a few!"

She clicks off before I can even say good-bye, and in another ten seconds, my phone vibrates again. There's Min reflected in a mirror, peeking out coyly from beneath dark bangs streaked with pink. She's wearing a red jumpsuit with a funky pattern that looks like a disco ball barfed up a sack of glitter. Another image appears—it's Min in a neon pink tank dress with grommets down the sides.

I can tell that she made both outfits herself. Min is obsessed with *Project Runway* and sews like a fiend. I text back that I like the jumpsuit and sigh. The truth is that I couldn't care less what Min wears. What difference does it make? I won't see the outfit in person—Min will probably be seated next to some weirdo who bought my ticket on eBay. I hope the eBay weirdo likes the jumpsuit.

I wander back out into the living room and sit down on the couch. It's this nice velvety fabric, and a very sinky sort of a couch, and it's very, very comfortable. A beam of sunlight slants through the open window, shining onto my grandmother's colorful oriental rug. A light breeze puffs through the apartment and Biddy walks to the rectangle of sun and perches there, like a sphinx, her tail curled tight around her front paws.

Three magazines are fanned on the coffee table, and I look at the headline of the top one. It's a *Time* magazine, and it says "Viruses," and I think about the world and how it has nothing but problems and diseases and melting ice caps and drowning polar bears and oil spills and how when I'm a grown-up all of the best jobs, like doctor and stylist, will be done by robots, and I feel a little down. Whenever I feel that way, I have to quickly look at the sky or something else that's beautiful and it makes me feel a little better. Like Althea says, a girl could get really bummed thinking about all of the stuff that's going wrong, and as you know, I do not believe in being bummed out.

I look toward Gran's window for one moment, but the sky beyond is still gray, which makes my chest feel a little bit tighter, and then I try to snap my mind onto some new thought. I turn back to the coffee table and notice two more magazines sitting there. These are something called *Newsweek*, which I have never heard of but which sounds very official. I pick up the top one—it has a picture of Ronald Reagan and the title "Reagan's Role." That's a little weird. I think maybe it's a "looking back" kind of article, but when I open the magazine, it's full of ads for stuff I've never heard of—Big 8 Cola? Casio watches? I check the date.

December 15, 1986.

I check the other one. Someone named Donald Regan is on the cover (Ronald Reagan's brother?). This one is from December 8. The virus one is from March. All 1986.

That qualifies as kinda peculiar. Why is Grandma Hildy collecting vintage magazines? Is she, like, starting an online store? I flip through them to see if there is anything in them about Cyndi Lauper. No luck. So I put the magazines back, trying to place them exactly as they were. For some reason, I don't want Grandma Hildy to know that I was looking at them. Is that weird?

I lie back onto the comfortable couch for just a minute and look over at the painting on the wall directly across from me. A serious-looking young guy holds his hand up to the glass that frames him. The look on his face is all hope and joy. But looking at that picture makes me feel kind of sad, so I kick off my oxfords, prop up my feet, and close my eyes. Wow, this couch is comfortable. It's warm in the apartment, almost stuffy, even though the window is open a crack.

A moment later, there's a heavy weight on my chest and I get this creepy feeling someone is staring at me intently. For a second, I feel like it might be the painting, but when I open my eyes, I see that it's Biddy. She's three inches from my face, and purring.

"Ugh—you're getting cat hair all over my uniform, you nutburger!" I scoop her gently onto the floor. Then I notice the clock, which freakishly says 9:50, which can't be right, so I look at my phone, which says 9:53, and for a minute I'm confused and wondering about time zones and time warps and black holes, and then I realize that I have fallen asleep and missed homeroom. And science. And part of Spanish.

Oh, no!

I stand up. Then I sit back down again.

I am sinking I am sinking I am thinking of quicksand and how the more you struggle, the more it just sucks you in.

*Another tardy means my parents get called in.*

No.

Nope.

My mom and dad can barely handle getting *dressed* these days.

Jeez, this couch is comfortable. I wish it really were quicksand. I wish it would just suck me in so I could just stay here all day.

And then I realize something: *It would actually be easier to skip school than to deal with a tardy.*

Because Haverton does not call home until ten thirty to follow up and make sure that you are supposed to be absent. If your parents get in touch before then, they mark you as excused.

And then my busy brain has this truly amazing thought that I did not even know was in there: *I have my mother's old phone—this number is on file. If I text the Haverton office, they'll think it's her.*

My heart is stuttering and my ears are buzzing, and I'm thinking, *I could do it. I could skip school. I could!* Because if you can't stand the heat, you should get out of the oven, am I right?

I'm thirteen years old. I'm in seventh grade. My dad is always telling stories about how he rode the New York City subway all over the place by himself at the age of eight back in the eighties, when the city was 95 percent crack addicts. And I wouldn't go all over the city, anyway. I'd just stay somewhere on the Upper East Side, which is all rich people and their small rich dogs.

I have never done anything like this before, and just thinking about it makes me a little dizzy. But what else can I do? I glance around Grandma Hildy's apartment. I can't just stay here. When my grandmother comes home, she'll have questions. And if she stays out all day, I'll be bored. My eye falls on a catalog from the Metropolitan's latest special exhibition. My grandmother leads a lot of guided tours at the museum—she is kind of a volunteer exhibitionist.

Beyond the window, the comforter of fog has begun to dissolve, and I can see the edge of the Metropolitan Museum of Art against a partially blue sky. *Museums . . . are . . . educational . . .*

The Met is huge. And very, very safe. I could easily stay there all day. Grandma Hildy always says that she could *live* at the Met.

I check my phone. The museum opens in six minutes.

I text Haverton. It isn't even 10 a.m., and I'm causing some potentially serious drama, but I'm not going to school today.

I'm keeping it happy—at the Met.

## CHAPTER THREE

# In which several important questions are answered and asked

HERE IS A VERY important question that has been on my mind a lot lately: why do I have so much junk in my bag?

I don't even understand where this junk comes from. It's like, okay, books, notebooks, pens—yes, that seems normal. But a mini watercolor set, a tiny *amigurumi* that I carry around for luck, three old movie tickets, about fifty receipts for random smoothies, a brush, three combs, five ponytail holders, a headband, my mom's sunglasses, my sunglasses, sunscreen, three lip balms, an ancient fossilized granola bar, a postcard I meant to send Zelda when my family was in Cozumel—I can find *everything* except my wallet. Which is black. And has clearly passed into some sort of space-time portal for wallets. Or maybe it has been stolen. How would I know?

Plus, the woman behind the counter is frowning at me and my head starts to throb because I think maybe she can tell that I am skipping school because I am still wearing my uniform after all, but I decide that if she asks I will tell her that I am doing an independent study project and I am fully and completely supposed to be here.

Uggggh. Now I'm next in line. I turn to the kid behind me and say, "I can't find my wallet."

"Well, I didn't take it." He's kinda huffy.

"No, no—I just . . . I didn't mean *that*." I really didn't mean it. But now I'm maybe suspicious. He is about my age—maybe a little older—and what is he doing here? Maybe *he* is skipping school, too, and is a *hooligan*. But then I realize that probably hooligans do not go to the Metropolitan Museum of Art. *Or do they?* Because, like I always say, you can't judge a book just by the shelf it's on.

He is giving me this look like I'm something dusty and sticky, like a raisin stuck to the bottom of a backpack, and it makes me nervous.

"I just can't find it," I say. "It should be in here." Then I giggle, but the kid doesn't smile. Like, at all.

"Why are you telling *me*?" he asks. He isn't tall—I can tell that I'm at least two inches taller than he is—but something about him makes him seem . . . like a tall person. And he has these really, really dark eyes that don't quite meet mine and are just a little bit scary. Not psycho scary. Just, like, in the way principals are scary, or rock stars, or, like, Santa when you're a little kid.

"I just mentioned it because you're, like, behind me in line?"

"And I had motive and opportunity?"

"Um, what? Is this, like, an episode of *Law & Order*?"

"More like *dis*order," he says, eyeing my bag.

"Just—the *point* is—just go ahead." I wave toward the counter, like, go, go, shoo, then I dip my hand into the bag.

He hesitates, and just in that moment, my fingers wrap around a familiar shape. "Yay!" I say, pulling out the wallet and holding it up.

"You found it," he says. His voice is flat.

I'm happy and relieved and then I feel badly all of a sudden because I realize that this kid was innocent all along and even though I never actually suspected him, not really, I feel bad for the nanoseconds in which I did, totally, suspect him.

I decide to try to salvage this awkward moment.

"So listen," I say to the guy. "My family has a membership. It's a plus one. I can get you in free."

"Because I look like someone who can't afford to get into the museum?" he demands, and I'm like, *whaaaaa?* I am literally speechless, and then he says, "The museum is free, anyway. It's pay-whatever-you-want."

I roll my eyes. Yeah, it's pay-whatever-you-want, but they have these signs all over the place with their "suggested donations" in big letters, that are basically designed to make you feel like a jerk if you don't pay them. So I was either going to save this guy some cash or save him some embarrassment, but clearly he doesn't care, either way. "Okay, whatever. Forget it."

"I'll try."

And I slap the membership card down on the counter and the woman gives me a little sticker and I tell her, "I am doing an independent study project," and walk off without looking behind me.

I head straight for the Temple of Dendur because there is something about ancient Egypt that really feels special to me. I think I must have been an Egyptian queen or princess or something in a past life, even though I do not believe in reincarnation. Because of math. I mean, there are seven billion people on the planet, and there used to be way less, so if reincarnation were real wouldn't the population be more or less, like, even?

The Temple of Dendur, if you haven't been there, is a really beautiful place. It is on the side of the museum, and one wall is nothing but windows looking out onto Central Park. The buildings are sand-colored, and there is a line of enormous and serious-looking lion goddesses who watch everything very calmly. Light comes pouring in, even on a cloudy day, and you can sort of feel the sun and think about Egypt under a wide, wide sky. And sometimes you can see kids playing or families walking past the windows, enjoying themselves in the park. Grandma Hildy used to bring me here all the time when I was younger, whenever I would have an overnight at her apartment. So when we moved to the Upper East Side I asked Daddy if we could get a family membership to the museum, and of course he said yes because he likes things that are educational and classy, which the Met definitely *is*.

So, actually, I come to the Temple of Dendur pretty

often. It's usually very quiet, and I like that you can go into the temple and see all of the graffiti that ancient Romans carved on it, which just goes to show that people never change. I took a very nice selfie in there, once.

I'm feeling kind of happy and reckless because I've never skipped school before and *I'm getting away with it.* I have a sudden urge to tell the small knot of German tourists near me that I am skipping school, and yay for me, but I am afraid that they might actually speak English, and then what would happen? I don't want to get arrested. So I decide to just enjoy my secret and the Temple. I kind of wish I had someone to share this with, but that just makes me think of Anna, so I close my eyes and Keep It Happy! for all I'm worth.

After I've soaked up some of the peacefulness of that place, I head back into the main Egyptian collection, which I also like. Egyptians had excellent taste in jewelry and gold things, which I also have, and which is kind of incredible considering how hard it was to make things back then. Like, they had to do *smelting*, which is a word that I know but do not really understand, now that I think about it.

I even like the mummies and the sarcophagi and the canopic jars, which are actually jars that they put dead people's organs in, true fact. The Egyptians thought a lot about death, and spent a lot of time getting ready for it, which I do not like thinking about but still find interesting. They did not believe in reincarnation. They believed in building giant pyramids and burying all of your stuff along with you. Which is a philosophy that I think Althea Orris could get behind.

Anyway, I am standing near my favorite sarcophagus when I hear someone muttering to himself. It's that kid. The guy from the line, the grouchy one. He's holding up his phone and whispering into it while staring intently at a small blue icon. I know the little statue—I actually happen to love it—and I happen to know that it is called *Winged Nut*, which makes me giggle because you can't help giggling when something is titled *Winged Nut*, even if you know that Nut is the Egyptian goddess of the sky.

He stops and looks over at me, only sort of above my head and over my shoulder. I am just about to say *Winged Nut*, and giggle more, but I feel like he is deliberately ignoring me, so I turn away and head out.

I'm going to the other end of the museum. Another floor. Grouchy Boy can have the Egyptians for a while. I'll come back later, when hopefully he'll be done with them.

CHAPTER FOUR

# Where I keep a secret and maybe discover one, too

The minute I walk back into Grandma Hildy's apartment I can tell she's home. The air has changed. I can't really explain it, but before the space was still, and quiet, and now it's just, like, a place that someone has been moving through. The energy is different, and my grandmother's perfume hangs there.

Also, she is sitting on the couch reading a magazine, so . . . that.

"Hi, Gran."

"Callie! This is a nice surprise!" She always says that, even though I drop by at least three times a week. "How was school?"

"The usual," I say, which I assume is true. I feel a little bad about hiding stuff from my grandmother, but mostly

I'm just sad that I can't tell her about the interesting things I discovered in the Met's Persian collection, which I had not looked at before today, and which I had also never known was the same as Iran, so that was very educational right there. And I can't tell her about the amazing painting I saw by Kay Sage—it's called *Tomorrow Is Never*, and looks like these falling-down towers, or maybe they're under construction, rising out of some misty water. And I can't even tell her my new saying (If you're having an off day, take a day off!), because I can't really have her knowing that I skipped school. That's sad, because I think that she might just be a little proud of me—especially since I went to her favorite museum—but she would also tell my parents about it, so that is out.

"How was tennis?" I ask instead. She is wearing her whites and her lucky gold bracelet, which is bright against her tan skin. Grandma Hildy is in good shape and her personal motto is, "Don't go gray—go blond." She always wears this pale shade of brown lipstick and a dab of Happy perfume, but she still looks like a grandma. To me, at least, if not to that guy on the street who called her a silver fox last week. It's a little embarrassing to walk around with your grandma and have *her* get catcalled. "What was the score?"

"Four to six, six to four, six to love." She smiles. "If I don't let Anita win one, she gets cranky. Are you hungry? Do you need a snack?" Grandma Hildy worries a lot about people not eating enough, and also about people eating too much. I think people in her generation thought about food a lot. "Would you like some *kourabiedes*?"

"Of course!" I say, because I love anything covered in powdered sugar, especially almond cookies, and we head into the kitchen, where Biddy is lounging in the windowsill. I give her a little scritch-scritch behind the ears, and she sticks her head way out, her eyes closed like *ahhhh,* as my grandmother flips the tape in her cassette player. I told you she likes antiques.

"Don't give her any treats," Gran says, and I give her this horrified, innocent look and say, "Me? Never!"

"I can't figure out why she isn't losing any weight."

"Maybe she has, like, a thyroid problem?" And then, thank goodness, the doorbell rings.

Which never happens in New York City, so this is a miracle.

Grandma Hildy goes to answer it and I trail behind her and out in the hall is a tall, leathery man with a silver moustache and a bald head. "You forgot something," he says to Grandma Hildy and holds out her favorite pink fleece and she blushes and says thank you and I'm like, *hm.*

He cocks his head for a moment, listening, and then says, "You're playing the tape!" which makes me realize, *aha! The cassette in the plant was from this guy!*

Grandma Hildy laughs. "I guess you're making me nostalgic."

"That's what I do." Then he spots me and says, "Hello there, I'm Earl!" His whole face crinkles with smile lines, even his forehead.

"I'm Callie."

"My granddaughter," Grandma Hildy explains.

"Nice to meet you, Callie," Earl says. Then he peeks out from under his dark eyebrows, gives me a wink, smiles at Gran, and says, "See you later!" before giving a wave and taking off down the hall. "Don't forget about what I asked you!"

"I won't," Gran says. Still smiling, she looks down at

the fleece in her hand. Then we spill back into the apartment, and she drapes it over the back of the chair and pauses for a moment, as if she's thinking of something. And then she heads back toward the kitchen without saying a word.

So now I am getting a little idea, and I ask, "Where were you this morning?"

Gran looks at me, her brown eyes sharp. "Why?"

"I dropped by before school."

"Oh, well. I was with Earl." And she smiles in this strange mysterious way that kind of reminds me of the time that Desmond stole Mom's eyeshadow and gave himself a makeover. He was three years old then, and when I found him in the bathroom, he smiled at me in just exactly that same way and said, "Do you like my glamour?" like he wanted me to see what he had been doing, but also wanted to be casual, like green eyeshadow was something he smeared on his forehead *every* day.

"That same Earl?" I ask, as though we are falling over Earls in our day-to-day.

"Yes, Mr. Johnson. He lives downstairs." And then that little smile again.

"I've never met him."

Grandma Hildy lifts her eyebrows. "I don't introduce you to all of my friends, Calliope." She laughs and puts two sugary almond cookies on a plate and I go and sit down at her pretty round oak table in the dining room just beyond the kitchen. She hands me a blue linen napkin and sits down beside me. In some ways, Gran is an old-school ladylike lady. She is a major cook and baker and always wears a dress or maybe "slacks" and she actually gets her hair "done" once a week.

Even though her theme song is "Girls Just Wanna Have Fun," my gran's idea of fun is flower arranging and collecting antiques and playing tennis and leading tours at the Met and keeping everything tidy and sparkling clean and her kitchen full of treats, so her apartment is a very nice place to visit.

Grandma Hildy has got it *together*, is what I am saying.

"So—Mr. Johnson is . . . your friend?" *Interesting*. My grandfather has been dead for ten years, but Grandma Hildy has never had a boyfriend.

"Yes." She sips her seltzer delicately, and I know I'm

not going to get any more information. This is just exactly how Min is when she talks about a boy she's into. She'll mention him five zillion times, but when you're like, *So, Min, what's up, do you like him?*, she's like, *I don't know what you're talking about,* and giggles and changes the subject.

So there's my pretty Gran, smiling and drinking a glass of seltzer with a slice of lime, fat with bubbles, floating in it, and I realize something mighty interesting, which is that Gran seems happy and maybe just maybe she is in *love* with a bald guy who puts 1980s music on tapes. Maybe he is her boyfriend!

It is a funny feeling to maybe kind of know a secret about your grandmother when everybody knows that grandmothers are not supposed to have love lives. It makes me feel happy, in a silly way, like one of the bubbles that is floating up through her seltzer, because I love my grandmother and I want her to be happy.

And it turns out, not all secrets are bad.

## CHAPTER FIVE

# In which our heroine (still me) remembers that *most* secrets *are* bad

WHEN I GET TO my brother's school, he is already waiting for me at the gate with his backpack on, although he is not allowed to leave until I sign him out. His eyes look red and puffy, and he stares straight ahead and I touch him on the shoulder and say, "Are you okay, Des?" but he twists away from me and doesn't say anything. Hm. My little brother is usually happy to see me when I pick him up on Mondays and burbling over with news like one of those baking soda volcanoes we made in third grade. So this is very unusual.

I figure that I had better sign Des out in a hurry, but I run into Rosario, and she tells me that her son, Felipe, just won a huge scholarship and is going to Hunter College in the fall and she is so proud and I am so happy because

Rosario is the nicest person in the world and also kind of broke (because being a nanny to twin six-year-olds doesn't pay what it should) and so of course I have to hug her and hear all about it. So then I wave good-bye to Max and Jack and David and Simon L. and Simon Y. and the three Sophies and Zephyr and all the rest of the kids in Desmond's class who are also in the after-school Funzone Program, and I wave good-bye to the teachers and finally we are on our way, holding hands as we walk up Park Avenue.

We are quiet for a few minutes, and I point out some yellow tulips that sprout by a tree near the curb. Des sighs a tiny sigh, so I know the flowers have made him feel a little better. The median is also planted with blooming tulips and the trees are nice and green, and we stand still and look at it for a few minutes as the traffic rushes past, because if flowers can't make you feel better, then things really are hopeless. Then a man with a pug puppy walks past, but the puppy is interested in Desmond's shoe, and if there is anything cuter in the world than a pug puppy I would like to see it, and Desmond bends to pet the puppy and the man says, "I'm trying to train him not to be afraid of kids, would you please give him this little treat?" and so Desmond takes the treat and gives it to the puppy and then the pug puppy is his best friend, and Desmond actually laughs, and who says that people in New York City aren't nice? Here we are, enjoying nature and flowers and puppies and Desmond's mood lifts like fog that is burning off once the sun comes out, and then we say good-bye to the man and the puppy and start back on our way, and Desmond is lighter, I can feel it in the way he is walking.

We take another ten steps, and Desmond says suddenly, "I hate Simon."

"He's one of your best friends! What happened?"

"Not that Simon. The other one."

"Oh. What's wrong with him?"

"He's a big, dumb bully! And he's stupid!" He spits the word, which is a word that our mother does not like for him to say. "Stupid Simon!"

I am confused again. "Are we talking about Simon Y.? The little Asian kid?"

"He isn't small. He's taller than I am," Desmond points out.

"True," I admit. Des is the shortest in the class because

he skipped a grade, and being tall is relative. "What did he do?"

Desmond holds up his lunch bag, which now has a hole in it. I gasp. "He tore a hole in Sparkle Pie?" I am horrified. Desmond loves his *Rainbow Puppies* lunch bag. That show is basically his favorite thing on this planet, and Sparkle Pie is his idol.

"So then I called him a canker blossom, and he called me a loser."

I groan. "Why did Mom take you to that performance of *A Midsummer Night's Dream*?" My brother has been using Shakespearean insults since last July, and I must say that they are shockingly effective, mostly because it's hard to know exactly what they mean. Like that: "canker blossom." How do you respond to that?

"Why would Simon even care about your lunch bag?"

"Because he is a stupid bully," Desmond says. "And now my lunch bag is ruined."

I smooth my fingers over the hole. It isn't the kind of thing that can be sewn, or glued. "We'll tell Mom you need a new one," I say. And then I stop and give him a hug, right there on Park Avenue. We're only a block from our house now. "When we get home, I'll make you some chocolate milk. It'll be okay." I know he can make it himself, but it's a nice feeling when someone takes care of you, instead.

"I love you," Desmond whispers into my shirt, and I remember suddenly how small a third grader who is supposed to be a second grader really is. I always think of Des as a full-size person, but—like Simon Yee—he isn't. I hug him tight. "I love you, too."

So we head home and, uggggh, the minute we get there my mom calls out, "Please go wash your hands!" and I remember that I am mad at her and at my dad, too. But there's nothing to do about it now. I have to eat dinner.

Desmond and I go and wash up using some of Mom's artisanal lavender-sage soap, and when we get to the table, Mom has put some weird kale-and-lentil thing on it, but also a loaf of homemade bread-maker bread, so it's not a total loss.

I love that bread maker. If we ever have a fire, the first thing I am going to grab is the bread maker, *that* is how good the bread is. And we eat a lot of it ever since my mom became obsessed with kale. Dad just looks at the kale and sighs and I must be predictable because I can see his future clearly and it contains a bacon-egg-and-cheese-on-a-bagel from the deli across the street. Usually, I would ask him to get one for me, too, but I will not do that today because I am still fighting off being mad, which is taking all of my energy. Keep it positive!

"How was your day, sweetheart?" Mom asks Desmond. He gives me this worried look, like he doesn't want me to say anything about Simon and the lunch bag, so I slather a thick layer of butter onto my bread and pretend that this task is taking all of my concentration.

"It was okay," Desmond says.

"Rose and Thorn?" my mom asks. This is a "game" we are supposed to play every night. My mother believes in these kinds of games because she has taken a lot of psychology classes and she believes that it is important to foster communication in a family, which is a good idea except when you have something you actually want to talk about and instead have to play this game. Anyway, for Rose and Thorn, we talk about the best thing that happened to us (rose) and the worst (thorn) and it occurs to me that I must be very careful and remember not to let anyone know anything about my day at the Met, and I have a not so very good memory, so I panic and blurt out, "Grandma Hildy has a boyfriend!" even though it is not my turn.

"What?" My dad looks shocked and repeats, "What?" His eyes blink like crazy behind his thick lenses, and his unibrow waggles up and down like a squiggly black caterpillar while Desmond shouts, "Yay!" and claps his hands and my mom just laughs and says, "Oh, Callie, don't be silly."

My dad takes off his glasses and starts to polish them on his shirt. "What makes you think so?" he asks. He doesn't look at me when he asks this, which makes me happy because now I can tell that he is uncomfortable about his mother maybe potentially having a boyfriend. So I say, "She was talking about spending a lot of time in Mr. Johnson's apartment," and then my mother and father exchange *uh-oh* looks and it's all I can do to keep myself from saying Ha. Ha.

"I'm sure Callie is mistaken," my mom says to my dad, and then turns to me to add, "Besides, it was your *brother's* turn to speak."

“Sophie S. taught me how to finger-knit, and there wasn’t any thorn, I had a great day,” Desmond says, pushing lentils around on his plate.

“Except that Simon Yee ripped a hole in your lunch bag,” I remind him, and then Desmond shakes his head at me, and I suddenly remember that *I am not supposed to say anything about that, because of Desmond’s earlier look*. Sometimes my mouth works faster than my actual thoughts.

“Why did he do that?” my mother wants to know.

“Because he says that Sparkle Pie is stupid.” Desmond stabs a lentil.

“I hope you taught him a lesson,” Dad puts in. He piles some lentils and kale onto a slice of bread and takes a big bite, and a lentil falls off the bread and into the thick hair on my dad’s arm, which is kind of disgusting.

“What kind of lesson?” Desmond asks.

“Desmond isn’t going to fight anyone, Dad,” I say.

“Nothing good comes from fighting,” my mother agrees. “Desmond, you must offer him compassion. You must visualize yourself as Simon’s friend. I’ll get you another Sparkle Pie lunch bag tomorrow.”

"You can't just get him another Sparkle Pie lunch bag," Dad says.

"Why not?" Mom demands. "I think we can afford *that* much, at least. For now." Mom spears a kale leaf on one tine of her fork and nibbles it, because that is the way she eats now.

Dad turns red, and I'm thinking *ooooooooo* because that was kind of a low blow, and that comment just sort of sits there for a moment, like it's munching popcorn and staring at all of us and wondering what is going to happen next.

"If you buy our son another Sparkle Pie lunch bag," my dad says slowly, "Simon will just rip a hole in that one. I'm not made of Sparkle Pie lunch bags, Helen. Desmond needs to teach that kid a lesson."

So I'm all like, "Can't Desmond just, like, take a brown bag?" which I think is a pretty smart solution but Desmond says, "I'll just take the old one. The hole is no big deal."

"Then you're going to have to teach Simon a lesson," Dad says.

"Why?" Des wants to know.

"Because Simon will just keep teasing you," I say. "Take a brown bag. Then he'll pick on someone else!"

"Why don't you get a different kind of lunch bag?" Mom suggests. "Spider-Man?"

"Spider-Man!" My dad agrees, as if this is a brilliant idea. "That's the perfect thing for a boy your age. Do they still have Spider-Man, Helen? Is he still around?" Which goes to show that my dad has not participated in the world in about twenty years because he has been working too hard.

"I hate Spider-Man," Desmond says. "He's creepy and you can't see his face."

Dad frowns and my mother suggests, "What about Iron Man? Or the Incredible Hulk?"

"He's just the regular Hulk now, Mom," I tell her, and she purses her lips and takes a long sip of water.

"I don't want that stuff," Desmond tells them.

"I know you love Sparkle Pie," I cut in, "but you don't want to get teased, do you?" It is very important to fit in, in my opinion, because school is survival of the fittest, so if you don't fit, you don't survive.

Before I went to Haverton, Anna told me, "Callie, if

they know you don't belong, they'll *eat you alive*," and if I am going to get eaten, I at least want to be dead. And I want the same for my brother, so I tell him, "If you take a brown bag, you'll fit in."

Desmond looks at me for a long time, his mouth in a little *O* of surprise, like I've slapped him, maybe, or stabbed him in the back. "I don't want to fit in," he finally says and he stands up from the table and walks away. Fifteen seconds later, I hear his bedroom door slam.

"Why do I even bother trying to make a nice healthy dinner?" Mom demands. "I should just stick to making soap!" She throws down her napkin and storms off into the kitchen for a glass of wine.

Dad pushes away his plate of lentil-kale stuff and stares at it a moment. Then he looks around the room, blinking at the expensive imported wallpaper. He shakes his head. "Maybe he was right," he says really quietly. Almost like he's talking to himself.

"Right about what?" I ask.

Dad just looks at me. I think maybe he is going to ask me a question, but he doesn't. My dad's not a big talker, really. It's like they say: silent waters run deep. Finally, he sighs and says, "Do you want to get a bacon-egg-and-cheese with me?"

"Sure," I say, because even though I am still a little mad at him, I think a bagel will help me stay positive. Also, I can't stand the thought of my dad going out to get his bagel all by himself, so I guess I'm not as mad as I thought.

## CHAPTER SIX

# In which a character makes an unexpected reappearance, and our heroine is like *whaa??*

THE NEXT MORNING, I wake up because "Girls Just Wanna Have Fun" is playing faintly beneath my pillow. When I pull out my phone, it is, like, one thousand degrees hot, and I wonder if it is maybe going to blow up or burst into flames before I can shut off the alarm. Min has sent me at least fifty texts, which is really only about twenty-five texts because half of Min's texts are just corrections of previous texts, like:

wheer r yo????? re you sich?

*sick

do you need soul????

*soup????

must plan frdy durng 19-min-breal!

*Friday

*during

*10

*break

Min says she does not like to use autocorrect, because that only makes it worse, but that is very hard for me to imagine, and I have a great imagination. I text her back, *Coming today*, and then get dressed followed by the usual: toast, kiss to Desmond, and out the door.

As I walk up Madison Avenue, my feet feel like I'm wearing shoes made out of bowling balls. I keep thinking about Desmond, and fitting in, and people eating me alive—which is supergross and not at all positive if you really let your mind go there. I wish I could talk to Anna, but when I try calling again, nobody picks up. I decide to leave another voice mail even though she never returned my phone call from the day before.

"Hey, Anna! It's Callie. I'm just on my way to school, you know, and I know you're a morning person, so I thought I'd try to catch you. . . . Well, anyway. Bye!"

When I click off, I have this yuck feeling in my stomach, and then I remember it's because I still do not have two hundred and fifty dollars for that concert ticket.

So I decide that I absolutely cannot handle school today, either. I believe it is important to protect one's mental health, so I take Althea Orris's advice and "manifest the outer reality of my inner desires," and that is how I end up at the Guggenheim Museum, which is also educational, but in a different way from the Met.

First of all, the Guggenheim looks like a giant white upside-down soft-serve ice cream and the inside is a ramp that goes around and around and around to the top. So that is educational right there, because it teaches you that people can like all kinds of ugly buildings. Second of all, most of the art at the Guggenheim does not look like art. Most of it looks like stuff Desmond could have done when he was three—like colorful scribbles on canvas or maybe a hairbrush dangling in front of a video projector—which is how you know it is very, very deep. In fact, when Desmond was three, he spent three months putting tape on the wall of our bedroom. Every day, he would add more tape, until it stuck out from the wall by a good foot in curlicues and ribbons. I was only eight, but even then, I knew my brother was artistic. One day, I know that I will see a twenty-foot-layer-of-tape ball at the Guggenheim, and I will say, "My brother thought of that when he was three."

So, okay, I get into the ticket line and am looking in my bag and in a very shocking turn of events I cannot find my wallet. I know that it must be in there somewhere and I am wondering if maybe it has an extradense core that somehow sucks it to the bottom of my bag, like these stars we learned about in science, when a voice behind me says, "Maybe you should consider a smaller bag."

And when I look up, there is Grouchy Boy.

He actually looks amused, and adds, "It looks like you could use a new one, anyway."

"It's vintage."

"Not everything old is vintage."

Great, now I am having a conversation with, like, someone who wants to critique my personal style while wearing a pair of sunglasses clipped onto the front of his shirt. Well, I'm sorry, but this kid is not Tim Gunn. "It belonged to my uncle."

"I guess he didn't want it anymore."

"I don't think he needs it. He's dead," I say, and when Grouchy Boy winces, I almost add, *ha!* but I do not because I am *trying* to be dignified.

"I'm sorry." He looks really stricken, and now I feel guilty because I didn't mean to make him feel *that* awful.

"It's . . . it's okay. He died before I was born. But I like his bag." My dad found it when we were moving, and he said I could have it. We don't have a lot of stuff from my uncle, so I thought, why not?

"Look—" the boy starts, like he wants to say something, but then he stops, like he isn't sure what. "I'm Cassius."

"I'm Callie. And—I'm sorry about yesterday. I didn't think you stole my wallet." Well, I kind of did, but I didn't want to get into *that* all over again.

"It's cool. I just—" He rolls his eyes and looks up toward the ceiling, way high above us. "Sometimes people make assumptions. When you're black," he adds finally.

"You're black?" I ask, and Cassius lets out this annoyed little laugh.

"So you're one of those people who 'don't see color'?" he says, making quotation marks with his fingers.

"I totally see color!" I say because I think for a moment that he thinks I am color-blind as in that I can't see green, but he says, "Oh, you're color-blind, but you still assumed that the black guy stole your wallet. *And* you assumed I couldn't afford to pay the entrance fee."

I feel like I'm on a roller coaster that just dropped before I had a chance to scream. Is this guy calling me *racist*?

*Wait*—the rollercoaster drops again—*am I?* Because I did kind of think maybe he took my wallet.

*But that was because he was behind me, right?*

*Yes!*

*I think.*

But I seriously had no idea he was black. I look at him carefully. I guess I can see it. He has big, dark eyes and black curly hair. His skin is the color of sand. "You could be anything."

"So I talk a certain way, and I'm in a museum, therefore you assumed I was white."

What? I'm sorry. Like he knows all about me and my brain and how it works or does not work?

"So—wait. First you thought I was a racist because I thought you were *black*. Now I'm a racist because I thought you were *white*?" Now I'm getting mad. "For your *information*, I *thought* you were Puerto Rican!"

Now he's a little unsure. "Are *you* Puerto Rican?"

I actually get asked this a lot. "No, I'm Greek."

"Oh." He looks confused.

Now I think that maybe he is worrying that maybe *I* think *he* is racist because he asked if I was Puerto Rican and now neither one of us is sure if we are racist or not, and maybe we are both a little afraid that maybe we *are*, but we don't want to think that because that's *disgusting*.

Cassius's eyes flick away for a moment. "What are you here to see?" he finally asks, and I nearly melt with relief. I guess he wants to change the subject as badly as I do.

"Uh . . . Mondrian," I lie. He's the only artist I can remember that's part of the permanent collection at the Guggenheim, and I don't have a clue what the special exhibitions are. Grandma Hildy and I have been here a few times, but nowhere close to the number we have been to the Met.

"I'm here for the Thannhauser collection." Cassius shoves his fists into his pockets.

"For school?"

"Sort of." He shrugs. "I wanted to look at *Mountains at Saint-Rémy*."

"Isn't that van Gogh?"

His eyebrows bounce up for just a split second. "You know a lot about art."

That kind of makes me laugh a little, because Ms. Blount—my history teacher—does not agree. "What, *girls* can't know about art?"

His black eyes go round. "No—I'm not saying that—" he starts, and then he sees that I am kidding and we both laugh.

"Listen, I'm really sorry," Cassius says, and he sounds supersincere. "I can be kind of . . . harsh."

"I get it," I say. Anna's the same way, to tell you the truth.

Then he surprises me. "Do you want to come with me to see some Impressionists? Then I'll join you for Mondrian."

And of course I say, "Great," because I think it might just be great, although it's kind of hard to know until you do something.

So we both head to the booth, and it turns out that we both have membership cards, so we get our stickers and head right up to see the Impressionists. I've never spent much time looking at the Impressionists in the

Guggenheim, because it seems kind of weird to look at something old-fashioned at this crazy museum. But they have this one Picasso that I really like called *Woman with Yellow Hair*, and as I'm looking at it, I say, "You know, this kind of reminds me of Lichtenstein. Because of the colors," and Cassius stands there with me and we both stare at it and stare at it, and finally he takes out his smartphone and starts whispering into it, and I hear him say *Lichtenstein*, so I know I have made a good point, and not a complete ass out of myself.

Then we go over to the van Gogh, and Cassius does a lot of staring and whispering into his phone, which is surprisingly okay with me. Most people look at a painting for, like, five seconds, and then move on to the next one. But these paintings took, like, months and *years* to make. The van Gogh is really something to look at, too, because the brushstrokes are so swirly and the colors are so vibrant and I like to think about how he was so incredibly passionate that he cut off his ear and sent it to some lady he liked as a present. True story; my grandma told me.

Once we have moved through the collection, Cassius

says, "Okay! Let's go do some work on your project now," and so I say, "Great," because I really like the idea of having a project and right then and there I decide that I *do* have a project and it is to look at Mondrian.

So I really look at Mondrian's art. I look and look at *Chrysanthemum*, which is a drawing of a flower that is so beautiful that it looks like it has a smell even though it is in black and white, and even though mums don't really smell. And then at *Still Life with Gingerpot I*, which is a little more abstract, but with lots of bold colors, and then *Still Life with Gingerpot II*, which is even more abstract and in softer colors. And then I look at *Tableau No. 2/ Composition No. VII*, which he painted in 1913. It's gold and gray and shell tones, and lots of uneven rectangles. And then *Tableau II*, in 1922, is a big white square painted very precisely, with smaller rectangles around it and a few points of primary colors that remind me of the Google logo. Going from painting to painting makes it easy to see how Mondrian's mind was working over the years—how he went from that beautiful, complicated flower to just a white square. He just stripped everything down to a basic shape and I think that Piet Mondrian probably had an apartment with, like, nothing in it. Cleanest closet ever, I bet.

Cassius and I stand there, looking at *Tableau II* for a long, long time.

"How did he get it so perfect?" Cassius says. "It's like a machine painted it."

"Right—Mondrian's probably like, 'The hardest part was building the robot.'"

Cassius laughs, and adds, "'Once I did that, the painting was easy! I just pushed a button and it took five minutes!'"

"Except a robot couldn't paint this," I say. "It could paint squares, but it couldn't paint *this*. It really . . . it says something, you know?"

Cassius nods, and I nod, and we stand there, looking at the painting and bobbing our heads, like we're hearing some kind of music until a security guard comes over and politely asks us to take a step back from the painting. I guess we are breathing on it too much.

We walk around the museum a bit more until my stomach lets out this loud, obnoxious gurgle, and I'm all embarrassed, but Cassius just says, "I brought my lunch—do you want to eat in the park?"

And I'm like sure why not because I have my lunch, too, and Central Park is right across the street.

We sit down, and he pulls out a sandwich. It's, like, an old-school baloney sandwich, and he has an apple and a bag of chips and so I'm happy because most of the girls at my school usually have some kind of artfully designed bento box situation packed by their parents or personal chefs or whatever. And I—who pack my own lunch and do not have the time or ability to cut a cucumber into the shape of a koala—usually have a bagel with cream cheese and tomato and a bag of these weird dried fruit things that my mom bought that are actually really good.

"So—what school do you go to?" I ask.

"I don't." Cassius is wearing his dark sunglasses, and I can't really tell if he is joking or not.

"You don't go to school?"

"I'm unschooled."

"Oh." I don't really know what to say to this. "I'm . . . sorry?"

He laughs, and he has this really silly laugh that's like a little giggle, like *heeheeheeheehee*, and that makes me laugh, and I let out a snort, which makes him giggle again. "So—wait," I say. "What do you mean you're unschooled?"

"Unschooling is like homeschooling," Cassius explains. "Except my parents don't believe in making lesson plans. They just think I should follow my passions and interests."

"Ohmygosh—is that legal?" I can't believe what I'm hearing right now. *Like, maybe I could be unschooled? And just wander around the city all day going to museums, like Cassius does? How can I convince my parents????*

Cassius laughs. "Yes. They're both college professors, so don't worry—I'm learning. I have to read a book a week and write a report on it, and I have to write a paper every month summarizing what I've learned in whatever subject I'm studying. So."

"A book a *week*?"

"Unless it's really long. For Dickens, I get two weeks."

*Ugggh. Disappointment. That sounds like as much work as Haverton.* I shift my legs a little and flick a piece of grass off of my knee. "I wouldn't want my mom grading my papers."

"Yeah. I don't get grades, but I have to discuss the paper with them."

"Oh, jeez, even *worse*."

Cassius laughs. "So—where do you go to school?"

"Haverton."

"Why aren't you there right now?"

"It's spring vacation."

He tilts his head back and sort of scowls down at my clothes. "Isn't that a uniform?"

"This is just how I dress." Hm. Let me just clarify that the uniform includes a white button-down shirt, a blue plaid pleated skirt, and knee-high socks. *Nobody* dresses like this on purpose, but it's like Anna used to say—sometimes a lie is as good as the truth, especially when you hardly know the person you're talking to.

"Since you're on vacation—what are you doing tomorrow? I was going to go to the Museum of Modern Art."

I say yes so quickly that I surprise myself. And then, like a crazy person, I add, "Just don't be surprised if I'm wearing the same clothes again tomorrow. I have intense personal style."

Cassius sticks out his lower lip, like he's thinking of

calling me on it. Instead, he says, "I probably wouldn't even notice." Then he looks up at the sky.

"Look at that one cloud," I say. "He's all alone up there." The sky is magnificently blue, and clear for miles. There is only one little cloud that looks like a Magritte cloud, if you know what that looks like—like a child's painting of a cloud, puffy and perfectly white.

"I wonder if he's lonely."

"'I wandered lonely as a cloud,'" I say.

Cassius's head does not move, but his eyes look at me out of the side of his sunglasses. Sidelong, that's the word. "You know the poem?"

"We just read it two weeks ago—don't get too impressed." This is true. I liked it, so I remembered it. It's not that hard.

Cassius turns toward me then, very carefully, very fully. Like he's looking at one of the paintings in the museum. I see myself reflected in his sunglasses—distorted, with a giant forehead and yellow skin. I have to look away.

"You're not going to whisper your secret thoughts into your smartphone? And write a report on me later?" I ask.

"You're a lot smarter than you like to pretend."

"I'm not pretending." And his comment sort of irritates me because I'm like—what the *heck*? "This is just how I *talk*."

"Hm," he says. He pulls up a blade of grass, then chucks it away and stands up. He brushes grass off his khakis, then smiles apologetically. "Look, it's been cool hanging with you. But I'd better get going."

"How come?" Now I'm a little mad. You can't just call a girl maybe possibly *unsmart* and then take off.

He crinkles his lips in this sort of embarrassed way. "I've got to find a restroom," he admits.

"Oh. That's easy." I stand up and sling my messenger bag over my shoulder. "There's nothing in this part of the park. The closest thing is at my grandma's place."

And so that is how Cassius meets my grandmother.

## CHAPTER NUMBER WHATEVER WE'RE UP TO NOW

## In which Cassius makes my grandmother cry

BIDDY LIKES CASSIUS RIGHT away. The minute I open the door, the cat trots right up to him and starts winding around his legs and looking up at him and giving him the big-eyed sputtery meow.

Cassius bends down holds out his hand, and Biddy sniffs his fingertips delicately, then rubs her face against his palm.

"Hello?" I say to the cat. "I'm standing right here?"

She continues to ignore me. She keeps rubbing up against Cassius and purring, like, *I love you, I love you, I love you!* I am, truth be told, a little jealous, but to be fair, I have seen her do this same thing to a table leg.

"Cats are crazy about me," Cassius says. "They can tell I'm allergic." He pulls off his sunglasses, wincing a little.

Grandma Hildy is, once again, not home. I show Cassius where the bathroom is, and then flop down on the comfy couch. Something hard pokes me in the back, and I pull a book from behind the couch cushion. *Iacocca*, by Lee Iacocca. Who's that? I flip open to the book description. It says that he turned around Chrysler, which is funny, because I did not even know that Chrysler was still making buildings, although I really like the one they have downtown. It's shiny.

When I riffle through the pages, a note drops out.

*Enjoy!*

*Love, Earl*

*Ooooooo. Love?*

I tuck the note back into the book and stick it back between the couch cushions. I don't want Grandma to know that I know her secret.

Cassius returns and stops by the buffet that sits right across from Gran's front door. It's crammed with silver-framed photos. He picks up the largest and holds it almost under his chin. "Is this your family?"

I go over and look. "Yes, that's my dad. That's my mom, and Desmond as a baby. That's me." I'm five in the photo, and standing on tiptoe to kiss Des's head as he sleeps in my mother's arms.

"Who's that?" Cassius picks up a black-and-white picture of a stern-looking man with glasses.

"That's my grandfather. Constantine."

Cassius squints, and twists his head. "He looks pretty serious."

"He *was* pretty serious." I shake my head at my grandfather's beak of a nose. He looks like an eagle, like a picture of him should be on the dollar bill or something. "He owned a plastic bag company."

Cassius's mouth dimples slightly. "That doesn't sound serious."

"Ever been grocery shopping?" My grandfather always said that when he arrived in New York City, he had three dollars in his pocket, and by the time he was thirty, *he was a multimillionaire!* He always said it like that, with an exclamation mark and everything, like he was hosting a game show and was also the winner. When he died, he left a big chunk of money to Grandma Hildy, and the rest to the Bookmobile Association. I'm not even kidding. At the time, there were all of these newspaper articles about what a great man my grandfather was and how amazing it was that he supported literacy and outreach to rural and underprivileged communities, and I'm sure all of that is true, but what I remember is that my dad spent, like, a week in bed. I was superworried that my dad was going to die of a broken heart because his father had passed away, so I started eavesdropping on my parents, and that is how I learned that my grandfather left my dad exactly zero dollars in his will. I guess he was afraid that money would spoil his son, or some such.

All of this is to say that my grandfather was a complicated guy. Complicated, and, yes, serious.

Cassius tilts his head back and studies the painting over the bookcase. "Is that your dad?"

"That's my uncle Lawrence."

Cassius's eyes flick up to me. "The one who had your messenger bag?"

"Yeah."

"He was handsome."

"He painted that. He was an artist."

"How did your serious grandfather like that?"

"I never really asked," I confess. To tell you the truth, people don't talk about my uncle very much, and I never asked many questions about him.

I don't really sleep over at Grandma Hildy's much anymore, since we live so close now, but when I did, I would sleep in my uncle's old room. Grandma made it into a study with a pretty daybed, but she left up one of his old souvenirs—it's an autographed photo of Cyndi Lauper. It's signed with two *X*s, and I think it's one of the reasons I've always liked her. My uncle liked her, too.

The door swings open and my grandmother walks in, looking flushed and happy, like maybe she has been running. When she sees me, she starts a little in surprise and says, "Oh!"

"I'm sorry," I blurt, just as a paper flutters past my nose. The open door has created a cross breeze with the window, and now a pulse of air rushes through the apartment, sending a pile of open bills and medical forms and whatnot on the sideboard swirling into the air and around us like a flock of startled pigeons.

For a moment, we are distracted. I try to catch a flying paper, while Gran stops a few from escaping through the door. Once it's closed, the breeze stops and the papers rain down on us, and Cassius drops to the floor and begins assembling envelopes, and for a moment we are completely distracted, gathering papers and other stuff to put them into some sort of proper order until we have them back on the sideboard in a jagged but somewhat pile-ish-looking pile.

Cassius hands Gran the final envelope with an apologetic smile, and then she notices the framed photo of my grandfather out of its usual place. Her eyes get a little stuck on the picture and well up. "Oh," she says, like she's catching her breath. She looks over at me, as if she is having trouble sorting her thoughts.

"I'll . . . I'll put this back." Cassius is awkward, but he manages to get the photo back into more or less the right spot.

"Thank you, young man," Grandma Hildy says a little formally, and I say, "Gran, this is Cassius." My grandmother gazes at me for a moment, and only then do I realize that it is maybe a little weird to have a strange boy in my grandmother's apartment since she is a little bit old-school and I am thinking that maybe she will think this is very and highly improper and whatnot.

I am about to jump in and babble something, but

Cassius reaches out his hand and says, "It's a pleasure to meet you, ma'am."

Grandma Hildy's eyebrows bounce up in approval at the word "ma'am," and I am impressed that Cassius thought of it because I never, ever say sir or ma'am or anything. "Cassius," my grandmother repeats. "What an elegant name."

"It's *the greatest*," Cassius says, and his black eyes sparkle and my grandmother laughs as if this is a joke and a part of me wonders whether I am missing something and I have to just add that it is kind of a little bit annoying to think that maybe my grandmother is getting a joke that I am not.

Grandma Hildy turns to me with a knowing little smile, and I must tell you that it's a *so-this-is-your-boyfriend* smile and I am suddenly seeing what my grandmother is seeing—a handsome boy with curly black hair—and those thoughts make my face hot, which only makes everything worse because nothing is more embarrassing than being embarrassed. And I can't explain anything without looking like a lunatic, so I say, "Cassius just had to use the bathroom. We were about to leave."

Then, of course, my grandmother says the most Grandma Hildy thing ever, the only thing possible in a situation like this. She turns to Cassius and asks, "Would you like some kourabiedes?"

Cassius looks over at me, and I give a little shrug. Because, of course, I want to leave. But I also want the cookies. So I am what Althea Orris calls *internally conflicted.*

"I don't know what that is," Cassius admits finally, "but I know that the answer is yes."

And that is basically all it takes for my grandmother to be crazy about Cassius.

## CHAPTER OKAY I WENT BACK AND COUNTED AND IT'S EIGHT

## In which our heroine experiences a memory

HERE IS THE THING about Cassius: he is elegant. This is what I am realizing as he sits there, eating the kourabiedes and seriously and truly making small talk with my grandmother. He asked her if her table was from the arts and crafts period, and my grandmother has gone off on a superlong tale about finding it at a flea market and refinishing it and then authenticating it and so on, and Cassius is acting like she is a genius and this story is fascinating and it's all just happening without me because I barely know what they are talking about. This table is just so basic. It's a circle; who cares?

Anyway, the whole thing reminds me of my old best friend, Anna, and last Thanksgiving, and then I get a sick feeling in my stomach and I try to make it go away by shoveling more cookies on top of it, but that does not work.

The thing is, I didn't like Haverton at first. When I met Zelda and Min last fall, I wasn't too friendly, because I just assumed they were snobs. They *looked* like snobs, with their shiny hair and all. I avoided talking to them. And to everyone else, for that matter, and my first few months at Haverton were pretty lonely. So, at Thanksgiving, Dad suggested that I have Anna come and spend a few days "in the city" with us. People in New York and New Jersey call New York City just "the city," which is kind of funny when you think about it, because even the people in Oz said "the Emerald City," though there didn't seem to be any other cities around, and there are at least three other cities that are *right by* Manhattan, including Jersey City. But whatever.

So my dad said, "Invite Anna!" because my parents were planning on having a few people over for after-Thanksgiving pie and coffee and the more you bite off, the more you can chew, as they say. So, okay.

Anna came over on Wednesday, and we had a super-fun time making popcorn and watching *Back to the*

*Future* (because she is also into retro stuff) and staying up late and all of that. But the next day, when it was time for Thanksgiving, Anna just put on her jeans and a sweatshirt, and my mom kinda had a minor flip-out.

The minute Anna went to the bathroom, Mom pulled me aside. "Callie, is Anna planning to wear *jeans* to our Pie Soiree?"

"I guess."

"She's not going to get dressed up?"

"Thanksgiving is pretty casual at her house, Mom." I had been over to Anna's house after Thanksgiving, and I can tell you that it is way casual, and involves football and bilingual yelling at the television set. It also involves "gobbleritos" for supper, which is something that Anna and her brother made up, which is a burrito made out of turkey leftovers and is *scrumptious.* "The only one who gets dressed up is her mom, and she's always dressed up."

"Look, I make soap for a living, and even *I* put on a dress. We want to make an impression. The people coming to our party are . . ." Mom couldn't come up with the right word.

"Rich?"

"They will be dressed appropriately."

"Appropriately for what?"

"For a *Pie Soiree.* Look, Callie, I need your help. This crowd is snobby, what can I say?"

"So?"

"Look, they hang out with Martha Stewart and Oprah, and we don't want to look like a bunch of slobs!" She took my hand. "They are already living the life we are trying to manifest."

"I was fine with our life before."

"Callie—"

"So—you want me to loan Anna a dress?"

"Yes, Callie. And we need to impress them—it's important for Dad's business, and for mine. They're from The Fund."

Somehow, whenever my mom mentions the hedge fund my dad works for, I hear the opening of Beethoven's *Fifth Symphony* in my mind: fund-fund-fund-*fund.*

"Some of these people might want to invest in Scent With a Kiss," Mom went on. "We don't want Anna to be *embarrassed.* Everyone else will be dressed up."

So what could I say? I said okay.

But then I had to explain the whole situation to Anna, and I could tell that her feelings were hurt. And I have no idea if she would have been embarrassed to wear her jeans at the Pie Soiree, but I can tell you that she was embarrassed in my green dress that was two sizes too big for her, since Anna is a twig and I am more like a log.

Still, though, she tried to be friendly and chatted with this one fiftyish woman wearing black leather pants and a black sweater. Anna went on and on about her favorite holiday movie, the underrated classic *Jingle All the Way*, starring Arnold Schwarzenegger, and the woman said that she would have to stream it for her grandchildren. So I thought that was very good, but later, my mom pulled me aside and told me that the woman was on the board of Dad's hedge fund and that Anna should not have been talking to her about *Jingle All the Way*. And I am not sure, but I think Anna overheard my mom. All I know is that she was supposed to stay the whole weekend, but instead she went home that night, after the Pie Soiree. She said she wasn't feeling well.

She left my dress carefully folded on the end of my bed. Anna hugged me good-bye before she left, but we were both awkward, like we had forgotten how to use our arms.

The good news was that my mom thought the Pie Soiree was a huge success. Two people said they might be able to help her soap company.

Anyway, so I am thinking about this as Cassius sits there, eating cookies and chatting about antiques with my grandmother. *He* is clearly from here—from the Upper East Side. My mother would probably love him. He clearly has "the life we are trying to manifest."

Whatever that means.

CHAPTER NINE

# In which the heroine's friends come to her aid (sort of)

WHEN I REACH MY apartment building, I nearly stop in my tracks because sitting right there on the black leather couch in the lobby are Zelda and Min. Uggh. Why is everything going wrong all at once? Hasn't anyone ever told Murphy that his law totally sucks? I try to turn around, but it is too late, they have seen me, and Min holds up a small brown shopping bag and calls, "Callie!"

"Hey, you guys," I say as they leap up to hug me. I am hugging them back and trying to peek out of the sides of my eyes to see if my parents are around. I am very lucky, because the doorman on duty is Ivan. His English isn't so great, so I am hoping he will not bother trying to listen in on whatever incriminating thing my friends are about to say regarding school and whatnot.

"What, uh, what are you doing here?"

"I made you soup!" Min says. "I used that recipe that Taylor Swift gave you!"

"Oh. Great. Yeah, Taylor, uh . . . she makes the best soup." I sniff the package. Actually, the soup doesn't smell horrible. I got the recipe from Tastealicious.com, which my mom uses a lot for recipes. She started calling the site "her friend," and then I started calling it "Tay-Tay," as in, "Did you get this recipe from Tay-Tay?" So when Min asked about my lunch last week, I told her the recipe was from "Tay-Tay," and Zelda was standing right there, and she said, "'Tay-Tay?' Like, Taylor Swift?" and she sounded like she was joking. So then I thought that maybe she was making fun of me, so I was all like, "Uh, yeah! Taylor Swift gave it to me." And Zelda looked impressed and said, "Cool, my dad has met her," and she definitely sounded like she *wasn't* teasing me anymore *at all*, and she was, like, jealous that I was soup-buddies with Taylor Swift.

So now I get more of "Taylor's" soup. "This was really sweet of you, Min, thanks."

"We missed you today!" Min is so cute and cheerful

and excited about the soup that she honestly reminds me of that pug puppy I saw yesterday with Desmond. It's always funny to see her with Zelda, who is more . . . house-cat-ish.

"How are you feeling?" Zelda asks.

"Better, thanks." I cough a little into my hand. "I was just . . . uh . . . picking up some medicine." *Hack, hack.*

"Where is it?" Min asks.

"It wasn't ready yet," I say. "They have to . . . mix it."

"I didn't know they still did that," Zelda says, so naturally, I'm all like, "It's artisanal."

Zelda lifts her eyebrows, but Min has already moved onto something else. She pulls out her phone. "I texted you the assignments." Min is, in fact, texting at that very moment, her thumbs working madly on her smartphone. "And now I'm sending you this hilarious—"

"Omigod, the video?" Zelda peers over at the screen. "You have to—"

"Juliette nearly *lost it* during lunch when I showed it to her," Min agrees. Min is always posting things on PicBomb and has usually seen every cool photo or video a week before it starts trending.

"And then she laughed . . ." Zelda shudders. She hates

Juliette's laugh; it's so loud that people always stare when she starts hooting. Zelda hates it when she feels like people are staring at her, which is kind of sad because she is so pretty that people stare at her a lot. Zelda has a difficult life.

My phone chimes, so I know I've received the assignments and the video.

"Watch it now!" Zelda urges, so I fake-cough into my hand again. I've got to get them out of here as quickly as possible, but the truth is that I'm really touched that they came over with soup, and everything. It makes me feel like we're better friends than I thought.

"I think I'd really better wait and maybe . . . uh . . . watch it in bed . . ."

"Oh, Callie, you poor thing!" Min wails, and when I cough into my hand again, Zelda adds, "Keep your germs away from me."

Min punches her on the arm, but Zelda says, "I'm serious! Placement testing is on Friday, and my mom will flip if I get sick and miss it."

I forgot about placement testing. That's an all-Haverton test in language, math, and science, in order to see who is going into advanced classes for the following fall.

"You'll be well by Friday, won't you, Callie?" Min asks. "Because the concert . . ."

"I'm sure I'll be well by then," I say quickly. I'll have to be, really. Because if I miss the placement test, Haverton will definitely call my parents in for a consultation, and that would be the absolute worst. "Listen, you guys, I should probably get upstairs. Everyone in my family is sick, too."

"Yeah, we saw your dad come in," Zelda says, nodding at the elevator.

"He looked *awful.*" Min's eyes are wide, and very serious.

"He got hit the worst," I say, which is actually a true fact. Just not about germs.

"Listen, Callie, would you bring the—"

"I'll bring the money tomorrow, Zelda. I swear."

"Okay."

Min gives me another hug, but Zelda just blows me a germ-free kiss.

I wave at them through the glass as they hustle outside. They wave back at me, and Min mimes eating the soup and rubs her belly. I nod at her, then notice Ivan staring at me.

"Soup," I say, holding up the paper bag.

"You are sick, Ms. Callie?" he asks in his accent that is from someplace in Europe where people sound a little like Count Chocula.

I fake-cough into my hand, and then say, "No," which, hopefully, could mean anything. Ivan cocks his head. I sort of have the impression that he thinks everyone who lives in this building is crazy, but he might just have Resting You're-Crazy Face.

"Well, I'll see you later, Ivan," I say, backing toward the elevator, which takes about five hours to finally land in the lobby and open up.

But it finally does, and then I am headed toward our apartment, with soup and a video, and for a moment, I believe that I really am sick and that I deserve all of this attention and special treatment. It's nice to get all of the good parts of being sick without actual vomiting.

Maybe I should try it more often.

Maybe I *will*.

## CHAPTER TEN

# In which the heroine eats some soup, which only leads to questions

"THIS IS GOOD," DAD says as he takes another spoonful of Min's soup, and I think about how the way to a man's heart is through his stomach. And then take a left at the esophagus, of course.

Tuesday nights are a kind of sad affair at our apartment, because Tuesday nights are when Mom takes Desmond to violin practice. So it's usually just me and Dad picking through the fridge until we both give up and Dad makes us cheese omelets. But tonight, we have soup and Mom made more bread in the bread machine, so we are living it up!

"Why did your friend make you soup, again?" Dad asks.

"She heard it was Taylor Swift's recipe," I say as if a) I'm not the one who told her that and b) that makes any sense.

"Well, it's good that she's learning to cook. I wish I'd learned how to cook."

"Why didn't Grandma Hildy teach you?"

Dad shrugs. "I was never interested. That was more Larry's department."

"Uncle Lawrence? I thought he was a painter."

"He was good at everything," Dad says. He scrapes his knife along the top of the butter, which totally drives my mother nuts when she's around. Like I said, we are living it up.

Cassius's question pops into my mind. "Did . . . did your dad approve of his being an artist?"

Dad's dark eyes lock on mine. "My dad?"

"Grandpa Constantine."

Dad spreads the butter over his slice of bread. Spreads it thin, scrape scrape scrape. "No." He pauses a moment and then adds, "He wanted us both to work for the family business."

"Why didn't you?"

My dad takes another spoonful of soup. He swallows, and then says, "I did."

"You did? But what—you quit?"

"Your grandfather sold the company shortly before he died. You were only three; you wouldn't remember."

"But—wait, why did he sell it? I thought you said he wanted you to work there."

My dad is chewing his bread until finally he swallows and I think he will answer me, except that instead he takes a spoonful of soup.

"Didn't he want you to take over?" I don't know why I can't let this go, but it just seems so completely unreasonable that it is bothering me.

"Things got . . . complicated." My dad puts down his spoon. "Look, you never really knew my father, so I don't expect you to understand. But he was a hard man. He wasn't even speaking to Larry when he died."

My mouth drops open in complete agapement. "Why?"

"He didn't approve of Larry's lifestyle."

"What does that mean?"

"Larry was gay, Callie."

I'm waiting for him to say more, like . . . *and Larry was also a murderer.* But he doesn't add anything else. "And?"

"And my father thought that being gay was a sin."

"But . . . I thought people were born gay."

"That's what Larry thought, too."

"Did—did Grandma Hildy think that?"

My father toys with his napkin. "I don't know."

"But she loves Uncle Larry! She has that painting up in her apartment—"

My dad turns to me and looks me straight in the eye. "I just want you to know that I will support you no matter what, Callie." He's looking at me really intensely, and I feel a little intimidated, but a little comforted, too.

"Uh, okay." There's just something I don't get. "But—Grandpa . . . How could Grandma Hildy have married somebody like that? Someone who would stop talking to his own son?"

"Callie." My dad looks so pained that I regret bringing it up. "Your grandmother never stood up to my father, at least not that I remember. I think she was a little afraid of him."

That's how dad always refers to Grandma Hildy: "your grandmother." I think it's maybe weird that they are not very close.

I never really understood why, but now I am starting

to get a little clue and there is a tiny little part of me that feels flattered that my dad told me all of this, but there is another, bigger part of me that is a little mad at my grandmother for marrying such a jerk and a little sad for everyone involved, especially my uncle.

I look down at my buttered bread. I've eaten most of it, and suddenly it feels kind of heavy and oozy in my stomach. "Do you want to go for a walk, or something?"

"I have to call the lawyer," my dad says.

"What lawyer?" I ask.

"My lawyer."

"What about?"

"Stuff about the fund. Severance stuff." Severance is when you're not working for a company anymore. My mom explained that "severing" means cutting something off, like someone's head from their neck.

I used to think that being a grown-up is all about being able to watch as much TV as you want and eat ice cream for dinner, but the closer I get to actually growing up, the more I've noticed that it's also about a lot of depressing stuff, like cancer and lawyers and severing.

We finish the rest of the soup without talking because

it's hard to change the subject when you've been talking about something really sad without seeming like a jerk. And it is also hard to keep talking about the sad thing, and maybe a little pointless. So what is left? Just soup and bread and silent walls. I think of a curly, twisty cloud, and try to hold on to it. Keep it positive, keep it positive . . .

The strange thing about other people is how impossible it is to know them. All of their thoughts are just this big, mysterious universe behind a locked door. My dad is sitting across from me, but I feel like maybe I don't really know him, *or* Grandma Hildy, *or* even Desmond or my mom. Not at all. All I see are doors.

I wonder if my grandfather ever had those same thoughts about his own son.

## CHAPTER ELEVEN

# In which I realize my evil geniusness

I HAVE HATCHED A plan!

Last night, I watched Min's video, which involved a guy on a Segway and a box kite and was very funny. Then I watched the video for "Money Changes Everything." And then I watched several Althea Orris videos, and I remembered about how I was supposed to think positively and convert my mental energy into two hundred and fifty dollars. And that's when I had an idea!

It involves breaking a rule, but desperate times call for desperate measurements and I need two hundred and fifty dollars and I really cannot show my face at school until I have it, so I am simply going to ask someone for the money. And that someone is my grandmother!

My father made this rule up years ago that Grandma

Hildy is allowed to give me and Desmond presents, but that the presents are not allowed to be money or gift cards. We are not supposed to take money in any form from our grandmother, not even a quarter for a gumball. When I was little I thought that this was because my grandmother was secretly poor and didn't want us to know, so of course I never took any money from her and once, when I was six, I even tried to give *her* five dollars. But now I realize that this is just a rule of my father's and does not make any sense much like many of his other rules, for example the one about how I should go to bed at 8:30 p.m., which never happens, by the way.

So I find a brown paper bag for Desmond to put his lunch in and give him a little pep talk about fitting in so Simon Yee will ignore him. I do a very smart thing and explain it in terms of science. It's called camouflage, and butterflies do it all the time, I tell him. Desmond likes butterflies, so I am hopeful that he finds this inspiring. It's like I always say, school is like makeup—it's all about *blending*.

And now I am on my way to Grandma Hildy's apartment so that I can get the money before I see Zelda, and if my grandmother does not have the cash, then maybe she can just write out a check or send the money to Zelda via PayPal.

Robert is misting the orchids in the lobby when I go in, and he scowls at me as usual but I just ignore him and head upstairs. Althea says grouchiness is contagious, and I don't want to catch it.

When I step out onto my grandmother's floor, I see Ms. Shaw stepping out of her apartment with a tiny little bag of garbage that must have about two tissues in it and nothing else. I am a little afraid of Ms. Shaw because she is always wearing a bathrobe. She claims to be a writer, but my dad once told me that this is just something people say when they are unemployed. Usually, I pretend that she doesn't exist, which works well, because she is pretty spaced out and may not even realize I am a real person and not a ligament of her imagination. But today, she seems to see me, because she says, "I heard her go out."

"My grandmother? You don't have any idea where she went, do you?"

Ms. Shaw shrugs. "1986?" she says, as if this is some kind of answer. Then she shuffles down the hallway, toward the door where the trash chute is.

1986? What kind of answer is that?

Shoot. This is no good. I consider asking Ms. Shaw if she noticed whether my grandmother had her purse with her but decide that this would sound suspicious.

Ms. Shaw returns from the garbage area, shuffling slowly in her bunny slippers. She's a little old—maybe forty or so—but she moves like she's older than Yoda. She should do some yoga, I think. Yoga for Yoda. "Do you have any idea where she might have gone?" I ask as she pushes open her door.

Ms. Shaw turns back toward me and cocks her head, like she had forgotten I was here. Then she says, "She's probably in her friend's time machine. 1986!" Then she slips inside her apartment and shuts the door.

Ms. Shaw needs to positive-think her way into some social skills.

But once her door is shut, I see the number on the plaque outside. 2085. My grandmother's is 2086. So . . . maybe she's in apartment 1986?

I head for the stairs.

The stairwell in my grandmother's apartment building

is rarely used, but it is always very clean and I like the way noise bounces off the walls. There are no windows, and today the light between floors flickers like a birthday candle refusing to light. I struggle against the heavy fire door on the nineteenth floor, and as it gives way, a rush of wind blows past me, nearly knocking me down. I can't quite figure out where it is coming from, but there must be an open door or window somewhere that is causing a draft.

I look down the hall and see a door that is slightly open and I begin to wonder if this is where the draft might be coming from. Sure enough, air seems to be whistling through the doorway. The number on the brass plate is 1986, with a name below: Earl Johnson. Oh! Earl! My grandmother's kind-of-maybe boyfriend. Now this all makes sense. I stick my mouth up to the door and say, "Hello?" Nobody replies, but I hear voices. One of them sounds like my grandmother. I do not want to barge in on a private conversation, so I just listen in a little to try to find out if this is the kind of conversation that is private.

I push the door open a little wider with one finger, and I can see just a sliver of Mr. Johnson's living room. He has a bookshelf that is very neatly arranged, alphabetically, with several copies of *The Handmaid's Tale* by Margaret Atwood at the top. There is a whole section for Stephen King, including *The Tommyknockers*, *Pet Sematary*, two copies of *Cujo*, and four copies of *Misery*. There's a section with John Irving. Below that are shelves loaded with classic VHS tapes, like *Back to the Future*, *The NeverEnding Story*, *The Lost Boys*, *Indiana Jones and the Temple of Doom*, *Stand by Me*, and *Pretty in Pink*. Nearby, another two shelves are completely loaded with small blue Smurf figurines, and below that are dolls in boxes: Michael Jackson, Rainbow Brite, G.I. Joe. There's even a Pee-wee Herman doll.

And I think that this is very interesting, because it almost seems as if Mr. Johnson lives in a museum. Like, his apartment reminds me a little bit of the Richmond Room at the Met. It is set up to look like a room in the Federalist historical time period, and this is like that, only it is set up to look like . . . I don't know. The 1980s, maybe?

I can see Mr. Johnson's torso and legs in a large cream-colored chair. I can't see Grandma Hildy, but I can hear her voice, and she's saying, "—where did you find it?"

"Scandinavia!"

"You're kidding."

"The internet is an amazing place, especially if you know what you're looking for."

My grandmother laughs, and says, "Let's play it!" and a few moments later, I hear a crackle of static, then the opening bars of some jazzy pop music—a weird blend of synthesizer and saxophone. Finally, a very familiar voice starts to sing, "Oh, oh, oh . . ." There's no doubt about it—that's Cyndi Lauper, but it's not a song I know.

"I haven't heard this in years," my grandmother says. I can't see her face, but I can hear her smiling.

Mr. Johnson rises from his seat slowly, like a bear waking up, and I'm surprised at how tall he looks. Then he steps forward, and I can't see what he's doing, but I imagine that he's holding my grandmother's hand, and a moment later, she and Mr. Johnson are dancing around the living room.

"This music makes me feel like I'm in my thirties again," my grandmother says.

"Oh, but you *are*," Mr. Johnson tells her. "When you're here, you *are*. It's called time traveling."

The hallway feels wavy to me, and I still have that

underwater feeling of almost drowning. The light feels strange, as if I can see the ripples over my head and sunlight is far away.

I don't know what to make of all of this, but it doesn't seem like the right moment to interrupt my grandmother. So I take a deep breath and skulk-toe down the hallway and slip into the stairwell.

I hurry down nineteen flights of stairs, thinking about Grandma Hildy and Mr. Johnson dancing in his peculiar retro living room. It is a little strange to think that my grandmother is friends with someone who lives in a 1980s museum. I wonder if she wishes that she could go back in time. Would Grandma Hildy really want to go back to a time when I wasn't even born? I can't imagine her in her thirties. What would she do if she could get a do-over?

My brain is so busy with this and other deep thoughts that I am three blocks away before I even realize that I forgot all about the two hundred and fifty dollars.

INTERLUDE

## In which there is talking on the phone

I HAVE STEPPED OUT of the subway and am hurrying toward the MoMA when my phone buzzes and ugh, ick—Haverton shows up on the caller ID. Crap! Why are they trying to call my mom? I texted them an excuse!

Is there no trust left in the world?!

I push the button and try to disguise my voice. "Hello?" I sound like someone who has been smoking for eighty years and now has a head cold. Just exactly *not* like my mom, but at least not like me.

"Hello, Mrs. Vitalis?"

I cough in a way that sounds like yes.

"Will Calliope be in today?"

"No—she's, uh—very sick. She—uh—she has bronch-asthma."

"I'm sorry, that's—" I hear keys clicking, as if someone is logging information. "It sounded like you said 'bronch-asthma'?"

Is that a thing? "It might be ammonia."

"Pneumonia?"

"Yes! Of course. Sorry—the connection is horrible." I'm standing near a construction zone, so I hold my phone toward a man drilling a jackhammer into the ground. Then a traffic light switches from red to green and a yellow cab honks like it's trying to use sound waves to shove people and cars aside. Satisfied, I hold the phone back to my ear. "She's going to the doctor today."

"All right, well, please remember to get a note."

"Ohhhhhhhhhff course. I will. She will. *I* will get a note for her because I am her mother, but she will bring it in." *This is going very well*, I tell myself, which really shows my commitment to positive thinking.

"All right. I do hope she feels better soon."

I hang up, thinking, *So do I.*

Seriously.

## CHAPTER TWELVE

# In which I learn to critique art stuffs

"ARE YOU OKAY?" CASSIUS asks.

"What? Yeah. Why?"

"You've been staring at that for about ten minutes."

"Yeah—I'm just . . . you know, pondering. This piece. It's really . . . evocative."

Cassius leans forward to look carefully at the art on the wall. Then he tilts his head back, looking at it from a slightly different angle. "That's a fire alarm."

"Oh." This is truly the biggest problem with the Museum of Modern Art, in my opinion: not all of the art looks, you know, arty. "This piece is really conceptual," I add, moving along to a stretch of blank wall.

Cassius squints, then tilts his head back almost as if he is looking at me with his chin, which is something I have noticed he does when he really wants to kind of consider my face. "The minimalism is groundbreaking," he agrees. "But I prefer symbolism." He points to the sign for the ladies' room.

"Look at this one." A bit farther on is an actual painting by the subject of my independent study project, Piet Mondrian. "See, this is no good. This is just, like, lines. And squares."

"Right. Where's the *art*?" Cassius demands. "We want to see more art like that fire alarm! More art like the blank wall!"

"Not these squiggles!" I gesture toward a painting by Jackson Pollock.

"A kindergartner could do that," Cassius agrees. "More blank wall!"

"More blank wall!" I raise my fist. "Keep it smooth!"

"Excuse me." A tall security guard with glasses and a paunch purses his lips at us. "I'm going to have to ask you to take a step backward." He watches us carefully until we retreat from the art. Then, satisfied, he goes back to the doorway, where he can keep an eye on us. Which is clearly what he is doing. I wave at him, and he frowns.

"I don't think he appreciated the complexities of our critique," Cassius says.

"Anti-intellectual . . ." I can't really think of the right insult. ". . . guy."

We move back to the Mondrian and stare at it. It looks like a city to me. Not like a skyline, but like a city viewed from above, with traffic and blinking lights. The whole thing is done in primary colors and feels like New York, and for some reason, I feel like I can hear jazzy music coming from the paining, which makes about zero sense. I look at it for a long time, and Cassius looks at it, too, with that weird Cassius-style I'm-looking-at-this-with-my-nostrils squint-stare. I really like it; it looks kind of tough, even though it is not easy to make Cassius look tough because he weighs like five pounds and most of that weight is probably hair. I tilt my chin up, too, but the painting's look doesn't really change. I wonder what he sees—if it's different from what I see?

Cassius turns to me. "What next?"

"Well . . . what time is it?"

"Time for a snack?"

"That's the time I thought it was!" I pull my phone

out of my purse. "Yes. It's 3:10—Frappuccino time!" Seriously, I cannot go too many hours without eating because my blood sugar goes down and also my stomach starts to rumble and then I get hangry. *A snack in time saves whine.* Note to self: inspirational poster.

We have on our little MoMA stickers that will allow us back into the museum, but I probably won't need mine because I should really head to the Upper East to catch Grandma Hildy "after school." It's only a couple of subway stops away, so it won't take long. I have enough time for a Frappuccino.

I check my phone and see that there is a Starbucks on Fifty-First Street heading east, so we head that way. I know that Starbucks. I have been there a few times.

About halfway to the Starbucks there is a little boutique selling fake-vintage stuff, like metal Star Wars lunch boxes and et cetera, so I think that maybe they will have something that Desmond would like to replace his *Rainbow Puppies* bag. I ask Cassius if we can go inside, and of course he says sure no problem. So we go in and it is a jackpot because they have *The Flintstones* and *Lost in Space* and Holly Hobbie and Wonder Woman and a

Smurfette one and a Hello Kitty and they even have some that are just plaid or just flowered. So I am trying to figure out which one to get as Cassius picks up a flowered teacup with a candle in it and gives it a chin-up stare.

A saleswoman hovers around behind him, kind of looking at Cassius nervously, and she asks, "May I help you?" but I can tell that what she is really saying is, "Would you please put that down?"

Cassius manages to translate this, too, and says, "No, thanks," and puts the teacup back onto its saucer.

"How much is this Wonder Woman lunch box?" I ask.

"Eighty."

I seriously cannot believe my ears. "Eighty whats?"

"Eighty US dollars," the woman says calmly. She is thin and has smooth hair and a smooth dress and smooth red lipstick and probably does everything smoothly and I just want to smack her.

"That's a rip," I announce. Then I say, "Come on, Cassius," and I sort of flounce out of the store, and because I have been practicing my flouncing, I think I pull it off.

We walk up the street and I am stomping, and Cassius says, "It happens a lot."

"What?" Like I don't know.

"They like to keep an eye on me." The corners of Cassius's lips are turned down, but his eyes are sort of crinkly, as if he is amused, or thinking, or mad, or a mixed-up smorgasbord of all of that. "Store owners. They don't trust me with the merchandise. But if I call them on it, they flip out and act like I'm crazy."

And I want to say something to turn it all into a joke, or something that will make it go away, but I can tell you one thing for sure—I have never, ever had a security guard tell me that I was standing too close to the art before I met Cassius. Now, maybe that is because there is something about Cassius that makes me stand closer to art than usual. Or maybe there is something about Cassius, in particular, that makes people not want *him* to stand close to art or pick up teacup candles. But I'm pretty sure that it has something to do with his light brown skin and crazy curly hair. I remember that time he got mad at me because I accidentally accused him of taking my wallet, and it makes a whole lot more sense now.

"I'm sorry," I say because I do not know what to say.

"It's because I look—Puerto Rican." He pulls open the

door to Starbucks, and I can't see his face anymore. Just his back. And I wonder about his expression.

Someone says my name, and who is standing right there with a giant cello backpack on her back? Zelda! "Callie!" she cries, giving me a hug. "You weren't in again today!"

She is holding a giant pink Frappuccino-type thing and suddenly I remember that the reason I have been to *this* Starbucks a few times is because it is close to where Zelda takes cello lessons and I have met her here before.

"Min was really freaking out and wanted to make you more soup," Zelda says, and then she seems to notice that someone is with me and she looks at Cassius and says, "Hi," and then turns back to me. "I thought you said you were coming in today!" She looks totally confused, and I realize she is staring at my uniform.

"I *was*! That's why I'm dressed for school—I just . . . My cousin is in town unexpectedly and so I'm showing him around New York!" I turn to Cassius and give him this crazy look because I did not even mean to just say all of that, but somehow I said it and I don't really know how to take it back or what to say next.

Zelda looks at Cassius, like she isn't sure what to make of this information, and Cassius says, "Yeah! I just love it! It's so different from—Cleveland!"

"Oh, you're from Cleveland?" Zelda says. "My grandparents live there! I love Ohio! Go, Buckeyes!"

For one second, Cassius looks horrified, and then he says, "I'm from Cleveland, Nevada."

Zelda's eyebrows shoot up.

"Go, Slot Machines!" I add, to make this seem more realistic.

Zelda is disappointed, but Cassius changes the subject like a pro. "We just went to the MoMA. And I think we're going to hit Chinatown later!"

I am impressed by this outstanding improv.

"Oh, I wish I could join you!" Zelda really does look like she wishes she could join us, which is interesting, because a) I did not invite her, and b) Zelda is normally quite shy. "But I've got cello . . ."

"Next time I'm in town," Cassius tosses out there.

"Listen, Callie, do you have the—"

"Oh, right! The money!" I paw around in my bag as if I might just find two hundred and fifty dollars in it. For some reason, I make this whole thing really elaborate, and I unsnap the compartment inside and rummage around in that, and then zip open the zipper on the front outside of the bag and look in there, even though I have never opened that compartment before because I thought it was just a decoration. The weird thing is that, for a moment, I'm actually kind of surprised that there isn't two hundred and fifty dollars in there, and then my fingers touch something, and my brain says, "Oh, the check!" even though that's impossible.

What I pull out is an old photograph. It's a small square with scalloped edges, and the color is faded. Three college-age guys lean against a railing. The tall, smiling one is my Uncle Larry. Next to him is a shorter, skinny guy with a shaggy beard and sunglasses, and beside him, a blond guy stands looking at something off to the side—something we can't see.

"Do you have it?" Zelda prompts and all of a sudden I come crashing back to earth and realize that this is a photo in my hand and I am never going to find two hundred and fifty dollars in my bag because I do not have two hundred and fifty dollars. "I—I must have left the check on the table. I didn't know I was going to see you—"

"No problem, no problem." She waves her hands and winces slightly, and I realize that it hurts her to have to ask me, and I feel guilty.

This whole situation sucks.

No—wait. Positive reframe: I will be so relieved when the two hundred and fifty dollars manifests itself! Which it will! Soon!

I tuck the photo back into my bag and Zelda gives me a huge hug and says good-bye, and Cassius and I stand in the Starbucks line as if that interaction were perfectly normal.

"So," Cassius says after a moment. He waits for me to fill the space, but I don't. Finally, he adds, "I guess it's not school vacation week."

"Right."

"Are you . . ."

"Skipping school. Yes."

The barista calls out a name, and a hipster girl with pinup hair and rolled-up jeans grabs her black coffee.

We make room for her, and then move back into place. "Why?" Cassius asks.

"Because I do not feel like going to school."

"Why? Are you failing something?"

"*No.*" I look at him with narrow, beady little eyes because I am very annoyed that he keeps implying that I am not smart when I am, in fact, very smart, mostly. Why would he think that I might be failing something? And what business is it of his, anyway? "I have some . . . other reasons."

"Personal, secret reasons?"

"Well, now you made it sound creepy. It's nothing creepy."

He tilts back his head. "Okay." Behind us, a group of slim European tourists enter the Starbucks and cause confusion as they stand there, studying the menu. Cassius doesn't even register them—he is still studying me.

"Stop looking at me like that."

"Like what?"

"With your nostrils aimed at my forehead. Look, some stuff is happening at home, and I can't deal with telling my friends about it."

"Maybe your friends would be understanding."

I shrug. "Maybe. Who knows?"

"You don't know?"

"I don't know them that well." I stare ahead at the board of drinks. It is almost our turn to order.

"Well, maybe you would if you told them the truth."

"Maybe that's what I'm afraid of."

"Isn't there *anyone* you could tell? Don't you have any *real* friends?"

I think about Anna, but my brain is feeling a bit twisty and turny. I know that I could tell Anna about my dad's job, and maybe even tell her about history class and all the trouble I'm in there, and I know that she would understand. But she would *freak out* over the two-hundred-and-fifty-dollars thing. She wouldn't understand how I could ever agree to spend that much money in the first place—and it would be pretty awkward to talk about. And she would want to know why I even care what Zelda and Min think. She wouldn't get it.

When I first started at Haverton, Anna told me I should watch out, because rich Upper East Side girls are mean. I think we have all watched enough television to know that! Even though Zelda and Min *seem* nice, I don't always feel like I fit in around them. And I don't know if

I trust them. I mean, what would they say if they found out I was just a girl from Jersey City whose dad happened to grow up with two members of the Haverton board of trustees, and *not* someone who got into this fancy school because Beyoncé wrote her recommendation letter? "I don't really know if I have any real friends," I say finally.

Cassius is silent for a while, and we are the only perfectly still people in the Starbucks. Everywhere else, people are talking, or checking phones, or typing on computers, or inspecting the display of artful mugs on the shelf along the wall, or frantically making espresso, filling the air with movement and spicy smells and energy. But Cassius and I are like rocks at the edge of an ocean, where the waves just beat and circle, moving in and moving out. "Friendship is not something you learn in school," he says, breaking the silence between us. "But if you haven't learned the meaning of friendship, you really haven't learned anything."

"That's deep, Cassius."

"Muhammad Ali said that, not me. He was a deep guy."

"Well, it just made me feel worse." I look up at the menu on the wall, so that I won't have to look at him.

What kind of saying was that? Althea Orris would never say anything like it.

"Think about it. Maybe it's time to trust someone. That's all I'm saying."

The line moves, and so do we, and now it is our turn.

There is a very, very small, maybe microscopic part of me that wants/expects Cassius to ask what the Big Flaming Secret is. But he doesn't. Instead, he takes out a ten-dollar bill and holds it up, inspecting it.

"Is that a fake ten-dollar bill, or something?" I ask.

"Nope," he says, and places the money on the counter. Then he orders a mint tea. That just seems so . . . Cassius. Then I order my Frappuccino, and reach into my purse. Naturally, my wallet has fallen into a black hole again, but Cassius just says, "I've got it," and pays for us both.

"You didn't have to do that."

"Why would I have to do it?"

"That's just an expression."

"If I had to do it, I wouldn't want to."

And even though this conversation is kind of annoying, I also kind of want to hug him and it occurs to me that maybe Cassius is the kind of person that I could tell about my dad's job and the stuff at school and everything. I don't know if he would understand, but he would be nice about it. I could tell him, I think, and then I think that maybe I *will* tell him.

"Carrie?" the barista asks.

"Callie." Why are baristas so pathetic with names?

He frowns at me, making his little goatee twitch. "Frappuccino?"

"Yes."

He hands me my drink and looks at the other. "Casual?"

"That's me," Cassius says, and I have to admit that I really admire the way he is able to keep his face perfectly straight, even though his cup actually reads "Casual" on the side. He turns to me and says, "Everybody knows I'm Casual."

We sit down and Cassius asks what I thought of the Mondrian painting we saw, which I really love, but in a totally different way from the way I love the ones we saw at the Guggenheim. So then I start talking about the paintings and my brain sort of switches gears and, in the end, I don't tell Cassius about my dad and the hedge fund and how I lied about a bunch of stuff at school and how I owe Zelda two hundred and fifty dollars and how—okay, I admit that he nailed it—I am also failing history. I don't even say part of it.

It's nice to think that maybe I could, though.

# CHAPTER THIRTEEN

## In which some stuff happens that I barely even understand

"GRAN?" I CALL OUT as I push open the door to Grandma Hildy's apartment. "Gran?" I have to shout, because probably my favorite Cyndi Lauper song of all time, "When You Were Mine," is blasting through the apartment, coming from the guest bedroom, which I think of as "my bedroom."

"Callie!" My grandmother strides from the hallway in her tennis whites. "I'm so glad you're here. Can you help me fasten this bracelet?" She's wearing her signature sand-colored lipstick that shows up against her bright smile as she holds out a tan wrist. She seems full of energy, as if she's still feeling like a thirtysomething after her visit with Mr. Johnson.

"You're going to play tennis?" I ask.

"I'm already late, and you know how Anita gets."

"Uh—are you—feeling okay?" My stomach feels cold and quivery, and I'm wondering if my grandmother suspects that I overheard her in Earl's apartment when I was here in the morning. My fingers are numb, and I can't quite make the latch on the bracelet work.

"Oh, give that to me, you're hopeless." Grandma Hildy's voice is playful, and I have this weird new thought that maybe *I* am going crazy and I was never here in the morning and the whole thing was a weird dream. Then Gran does a little dance and sings along with the song, "I love you more than I did when you were mine!"

My bag buzzes against my leg, and when I reach inside, my fingers close on the photo I found earlier. I pull it out and my grandmother plucks it from my fingers as I dig around again, finally finding my phone. "Hello?"

"Why aren't you answering your texts?" It's my mom.

"What? I was in the subway." Crap—I just realized I was supposed to be at school, not on the subway! *Delete! Delete!*

"Subway? What? Callie—I need you to go get Desmond."

"Why? Funzone just started."

"I'm in the middle of a Skype with a client and your brother is being sent home for hitting some boy in the head with a lunch bag."

"What?" This is so far from the realm of possibility that I assume that I have misheard her. "Where's Dad?

"With the lawyer. Look, you need to get Dezzie right away!"

"Okay, I—okay, I'm going." I click off. "I have to go pick up Desmond right away . . ." When I look up, I notice that Grandma Hildy has gone still. She stares at the photo she took from me—the one I found in my bag. Her lips have fallen slightly open. "It's Larry," she says softly. In the background, the last line of the song echoes, trailing off as it nears the end. Then it begins again abruptly; it's on repeat.

I twist my head to get a better look at the photo. "Yeah—and two other guys."

Grandma Hildy points. "Your father."

"Seriously?" I look more closely, and realize that she is right—the scrawny dude with the beard and the sunglasses . . . remove the beard, remove the sunglasses, add gray to the hair, add forty pounds . . . "Who is the other guy?"

My grandmother sighs. "Stephen," she says, but she doesn't sound sure.

"You don't know?"

"I never met him. I just heard about him. He was your uncle's friend." She places the photo on the sideboard, not even asking if she can keep it. She can, of course. I'm just saying that she did not ask.

*Ugh!* A thought occurs to me, and I blurt out, "Gran, can I have two hundred and fifty dollars?"

Grandma Hildy blinks. "Why?" she asks.

"Dad said I could go to this concert two months ago, so I told my friend to go ahead and buy tickets, so her mom did, but now we can't really afford it, but it's kind of too late—"

"Your father isn't going to honor his commitment?"

"Well, since the hedge fund is shutting down—"

"The hedge fund is closing?" Grandma Hildy's face goes rigid, like a mask, and I realize OHMYGODMAYBETHAT'SASECRET.

But nobody told me! I mean, I can barely keep a secret

when I *know* it's a secret! Okay, okay—quick, I need a positive reframe!

Um . . . struggling . . .

Grandma is looking at me like a hawk. "I'll get my checkbook," she says at last, and I am left standing there, kind of gasping.

Biddy walks out from the kitchen and winds herself around my legs. "You are so lucky to be a cat," I tell her, and a moment later my grandmother comes out with her purse over her arm. She finishes signing the check and hands it to me.

Relief just pours through me like some kind of cleansing Bath and Body Works foaming bath wash, only without the gross smell. "Thank you," I whisper.

I hug her, and she says, "Now go get your brother," so I go out into the hallway, and she follows. I call for the elevator, and step inside. "Are you coming? Should I wait for you?" I am offering to be polite, but I'm really kind of freaking out about Desmond.

"I still have to put on my socks and sneakers and get my water bottle ready. You go ahead."

"Bye, Gran."

"Bye, sweetheart."

"Please don't tell Dad about this," I beg as I press the button for the first floor. I look down at the check again, and just as the door is closing, I notice the date Grandma Hildy wrote on the check—April 24, 1986.

## CHAPTER FOURTEEN

# In which: bullies; ugh!

SOMETIMES I THINK THAT it is not that surprising that famous people are always suffering from exhaustion because I think that I am suffering from exhaustion and my life is just normal. I do not even have time to freak out about the fact that I can't cash a check from 1986 because I have to pick up my little brother, who apparently has beaten someone up. Do these things even count as first-world problems?

I rub my right arm with my left because this place is over-air-conditioned. I am seated on a dark leather chair just outside the principal's office at Desmond's school. The seat is both poufy and uncomfortable somehow, like they shoved too much stuffing inside it. This office looks like a hunting lodge, only without the deer heads on the walls.

I guess it would be a little weird for an elementary school principal to be surrounded by a bunch of dead animals. It might seem a bit spooky. This office is sort of accomplishing the spooky thing, even without the decapitated animals, though, and I'm just sitting in the reception area.

"You can go in, Callie," Mrs. Lewis tells me. I can't see her over the partition that separates her desk from the seating area because Mrs. Lewis is about four feet tall even when she is standing up. She has worked at the school for over thirty years, and everybody knows she basically runs the place.

"Thanks, Mrs. Lewis," I say, and I give a little knock on the door and then push it open.

Desmond is sitting on another one of those god-awful chairs, facing the principal, who looks like—and I mean this in the nicest possible way—a toad who has been drinking too much coffee. He's pale, and bald, and his neck is somehow wider than his cheeks, and the pouches under his eyes look like they are filled with grape juice, and, basically, he looks like he has had the kind of week that I have been having, only for about ten years. He takes out a handkerchief and coughs into it, then sticks it back into the pocket of his jacket.

Desmond's lunch bag is on the desk, Exhibit A.

I turn to Desmond, whose face is red and blotchy, but not like he has been crying. More like he is trying not to scream. "Are you okay?" I ask.

"Callie Vitalis?" The principal stands up and shakes my hand, and I'm surprised by his tiny fingers and how slightly cold and almost wormy they feel. "Thank you for coming down. I'm Sal Becker."

"I met you at Family Night," I remind him.

"Oh, yes. Of course." He drops back into his tall brown leather office chair, which lets out a sigh. "I'm releasing Desmond to you, as neither of your parents are available to pick him up, but please let them know that they should call the office and schedule an appointment as soon as possible."

"So what happened?"

"I can't give you that information," Mr. Becker says. He coughs delicately into his handkerchief.

I look over at Desmond, who rolls his eyes.

"Okay." In a way, I am super-relieved not to have to get into a whole discussion about what happened at school because my brain feels very much like a sponge that has been dropped in the ocean, and another ounce of information is just going to float around me like . . . I don't know. Like extra water that can't get into a sponge.

I guess I'm too tired to metaphor right now.

Des stands up, and I reach for the lunch bag, but Mr. Becker puts his hand on it to stop me. "I think we'll just leave this here." He gives me this tight little smile and clears his throat.

"Oh. Okay," I say, and Desmond gives me this *how could you?* look, but what am I supposed to do? Grab the lunch bag and bean the principal with it? Desmond stomps out of the principal's office, and I kind of wince at Mr. Becker like *I'm sorry* and close the door behind me. When we leave, I hear him hacking into his handkerchief again, as if maybe he's allergic to dealing with students.

Mrs. Lewis is standing by the copy machine. "Where's your lunch bag?" she asks Desmond, who just points at the door. "Hm." Mrs. Lewis purses her lips and glances at Mr. Becker's door like she might just barge in there. I really wish *she* were the principal.

I don't say anything to my brother until we are outside. "Desmond, what the heck?"

My little brother bursts into tears, and I try to hug

him but he pushes me away. "I'm not sad, I'm just mad!" He stomps his foot and bursts into tears all over again.

"What happened?"

"Simon Yee was making fun of my lunch bag and he tried to grab it away from me. I wouldn't let him have it, and then I let go really suddenly, and he bashed himself in the forehead. The zipper cut his eyebrow, so blood was streaming down his face. I wish it had poked his eye out! I would've stomped on it!"

"Desmond!" I seriously have never heard my brother this angry. Never. Ever. About anything.

He looks a little guilty, then kind of gets over it and looks mad again. "That fustilarian!"

Oh, boy. More Shakespeare. "Did you tell Mr. Becker the whole story?"

"Yes."

"And what did he say?"

"He said that it was my fault for bringing the lunch bag to school. He said I provoked Simon."

"Well, he's kind of right. Why didn't you just use the paper bag I gave you?"

Desmond shakes his head. "When I woke up, I was just

so—mad. I was going to take the paper bag, but then I saw Sparkle Pie on the counter and I grabbed it. It didn't even have anything in it, so I put in a water bottle and an apple. I guess the water bottle was heavy, and that's why Simon got hurt when he whacked himself." Desmond shuffles down the asphalt. It's four thirty—half an hour before Desmond's after-school program usually ends. It does not seem to make much of a difference as to how many people are on the sidewalk, though. One of the interesting things about Manhattan is that people are always out walking around on the streets. Everyone seems to have jobs at odd times, or maybe nobody has jobs, or they all have jobs that they do not care about.

As usual, there are many possible possibilities.

Desmond is staring at the ground, and I know that his mind has wandered off just like mine has. I do not think that he is so angry anymore, so I reach out for his hand and he lets me hold it. I feel a surge of love for my little brother, which is a very positive thing.

"Tomorrow," I say gently, "please just buy yourself a hot lunch."

Desmond's mouth snaps open, like he is going to say

something angry, but he stops himself. “Fine.”

“Thanks.”

“I’ll have to, anyway. My lunch bag is in Mr. Becker’s office.”

“That’s a good point.” I squeeze his hand, and I guess we both feel a little better. I’m not so mad anymore. The truth is that even though I think the principal was being unfair, I think that maybe he did the right thing. Desmond will just buy his lunch tomorrow, and Simon Yee will hopefully move on to bothering someone else.

And then, at least *one* of my weird problems will be solved.

## CHAPTER FIFTEEN

# In which I make a mess

So WHEN WE GOT home, my mom went all mental, and was like, "DO YOU KNOW HOW HARD IT IS TO CRAFT ARTISANAL SOAP WHEN YOUR OWN SON IS A DELINQUENT???!!!!" and there was a lot of yelling because my mom only has two clients who actually carry her soap in their stores, and as she says, it is VERY STRESSFUL TO TRY TO BUILD A BUSINESS.

Desmond was defensive and refused to say he was sorry about Simon and then my mom was like, "I CAN'T DEAL WITH MAKING DINNER!" and when we all just stood there like uhhhhhhh, she shouted, "CAN I JUST GET A LITTLE HELP AROUND HERE!?" and then she sent Desmond to his room and went to lie down.

It was quite the dramatic monologue, and that is why

Dad and I are at Whole Foods picking up a rotisserie chicken and some other Whole Foods-y kinds of things. My dad is staring at the display of deli items, like it is some kind of intelligence test that we are both failing. "Why can't they just have potato salad?" he asks.

"They have some." I point.

"I mean *normal* potato salad." He reads the description. "Who the hell wants tarragon in their potato salad?" He puts a hand to his forehead, like the potato salad has just made him completely exhausted. "And why does the closest grocery store have to be so *expensive*?"

"Because it's Whole Foods?"

He sighs. "It's still cheaper than eating out, I guess."

"We'll take half a pound of this," I tell the guy, pointing to the potato salad, and then I turn to my dad. "It's probably good. I mean, it's potatoes."

"Okay."

"And we'll just get a bag of lettuce and throw dressing on it."

"Okay."

"And maybe some fruit for, like, dessert. Desmond likes cherries. They have some."

"Okay."

I just take charge of the shopping trip and gather everything into the basket and my dad kind of trails around behind me and it's a little depressing, to tell you the truth. So I am standing there in the produce aisle, trying to find a positive reframe while I grab the cherries, but my dad spots a Special of the Week, so we get grapes instead and head to the checkout line.

There is a rack of magazines beside us. A very minimalist living room is on the cover of *Conscious Furbishings*, and my heart starts thumping madly. "Isn't it great how 1980s stuff is coming back?"

My dad looks at the magazine. "I think that style is more 1950s."

"But people really like 1980s stuff."

"Oh."

"Like Smurf collections are really in right now."

"Hm," Dad says. He takes out his wallet and pays. Then we grab our bags and walk out of Whole Paycheck, and up Lexington Avenue. "Is there something you want to talk to me about, Callie?"

"Well . . . I just. Remember Grandma Hildy's friend Mr. Johnson?"

Dad's face is blank for a moment, and then he nods.

"I kind of went by his apartment today, and it was . . ." I'm trying to think of the right words. "Well, it was weird."

Dad's eyebrows shoot up, and he looks a little horrified.

"Nothing bad happened!" I say quickly. "I didn't even go inside. I was just looking for Grandma Hildy, and she was there—it's just . . . like I said, it was a little weird."

My dad tips his head a little, but does not say anything.

"It's—well, the whole place is *very* 1980s."

"I thought you said that was in fashion."

"Um . . . well, it's kind of . . . It's just got an almost *museum-like* vibe? Like the Richmond Room?"

Dad looks blank.

"In the American wing?"

More blankness.

"At the Met. Only, instead of the 1800s, it's, like, the 1980s. All the . . . stuff . . . is from then."

A little frown wriggled on my dad's lips. "So—"

"I don't know. It just seemed weird."

"And her friend—what's his name?"

"Earl Johnson."

"Well—what about him?"

"Like what?"

"Like . . . did *he* seem weird?" My dad sounds stressed, and I feel like I can actually see his hair falling out of his scalp as we walk along.

"I don't know. I mean, he seems *nice*. Look, it was just odd, that's all." I don't tell him Ms. Shaw said the apartment was a time machine or that everything in it—even the magazines—was from 1986. And I don't mention about Grandma Hildy feeling younger and writing the wrong date on the check, because then I would have to mention the check, which is not happening.

I really regret bringing it up at all. I don't have any idea why I did. I felt like I wanted to talk about it, but then I started and I found out I didn't, so there you go. How can I tell my dad that Grandma Hildy was *dancing*, and that it seemed like she was *someone else*, and I felt like I was *underwater*? You can't tell dads stuff like that, or at least I've never heard of it.

Dad stops right in front of me to look into my face, which makes me want to run into the frozen yogurt store next to us and hide behind the toppings bar. "Is there something else you want to say?" he asks in this way that seems to say that I had better say something.

"Well . . . I think Mr. Johnson might want to . . . date . . . Grandma. That's all. Maybe." I wince a little. I look into the window, wishing we could just talk about frozen yogurt toppings. But my dad presses on.

"Well, I think that if your grandmother wants to *date*, then she should. She seems a lot happier now than she ever was when my father was alive."

"Really?" I think about that. My grandfather died when I was three. I don't really remember what my grandmother was like before then.

"Look, she's a grown woman. It doesn't have anything to do with me."

Dad looks at me a moment longer, and I say, "Should we get some frozen yogurt?" in the perkiest voice I can muster.

Dad blinks slowly, as if he is finished inspecting my face. He doesn't say anything, but he turns, and we both begin walking toward home.

Back at the apartment, dinner is pretty tense. Desmond stays in his room and my mom just picks at her chicken. My dad stabs at his salad but doesn't actually eat much. I make up for everyone else by snarfing ALL OF THE POTATO SALAD, because that stuff is awesome. Basically the best thing I've ever had, true story. I guess it's the tarragon.

Mom goes to the bedroom to plan her monthly mindfulness workshop, and I clear off the table because I am not going to go make Desmond do it, even though it is technically his turn, and my dad looks exhausted and stressed.

I'm busy in the kitchen and do not hear him get up and leave of the room, but when I walk down the hallway later, I hear my mom saying, "—if they do get married?"

My dad murmurs; I can't really hear what he is saying, but it ends in, "—her choice."

Mom: "What if he's just after her money?"

Suddenly, my father's voice gets very crisp. "It doesn't matter; that money is for *her*, not me. Dad made that very clear when he said that I was too weak to handle responsibility, remember?"

Mom: "George, what if this lawsuit drags on? We could be wiped out. How are we going to send the kids to college? How are we going to retire?"

Dad: "I thought we were going to retire on your *soap empire*."

Mom: "That was mean."

Dad: "I'm sorry."

Mom: "If I had known about the hedge fund, I never would have left social work. I never would have left New Jersey!"

Dad: "I know. I know; I'm sorry."

Mom: "New York City was *your* dream, not mine—you were the one who wanted to show your parents that you could make it on your own—"

Dad: "That's just it, Helen—I would rather starve than take money from her after what they did to Larry. If I succeed or fail, it's without them—just like Larry."

Mom: "Well, what does she say about the fund?"

Dad: . . .

Mom: "Oh my god, you haven't told her? Have you told her about the lawsuit? Are you going to wait until she reads about it in the newspaper, George?"

And then there is more silence, and it is a silence that stretches on and on. It's a silence that is deep, and somehow final, and it makes me feel strangely embarrassed, even though my parents don't know that I am listening to them. It's like that phrase—if a tree falls in the forest and nobody hears it, does it make a sound? And if the tree thinks it's alone, and thinks it's not making a sound, but somebody hears it anyway, does it count?

I'm seriously asking, because I think that might be good on a T-shirt.

I creep away toward my room, feeling sick to my stomach, and a little frightened, and wondering what "they" did to Larry. "They," as in, my grandparents? "They," as in, Grandma Hildy?

And—what lawsuit?

Do you know those pictures that you can see two ways? Like, it looks like an old lady to half the people, and to the other half, it looks like a young one? Or, like, is it a pineapple or the Statue of Liberty—or whatever?

For the first time ever, I wonder why my father barely ever talks to my grandmother. I wonder why we're not supposed to take money from her. That has always just been the way it is. Now I see that maybe there's more to it than I thought.

And I wonder why I never wondered about it before.

## CHAPTER WHATEVER

# In which blah, blah, blah. I can't even think of a synopsis right now–just read it yourself, okay?

IT'S ALMOST BEDTIME, BUT I know I won't be able to sleep. My brain is swirling, and that is making me think of those cyclones you hear about, the ones that pick up a car and toss it fifty feet and then crush a building and basically destroy everything and leave the whole town crying on TV.

I mean, according to Althea Orris, those people's bad thoughts manifested that mess, so I am a little worried that my out-of-control brain might cause some serious brain damage!

So I decide to stop swirling and distract myself. My computer is sleek and silver and the exact same kind that every other girl in my school has, and I think it is so pretty and I really like typing on it. I do my homework on it, of course, but I also like to write stories. Sometimes I pretend that I am CEO of a fashion house or something, and I type up descriptions for the imaginary dresses for our catalog. Like this:

"Made from artisanal silk fibers found on the banks of the Nile River, this Isis-inspired goddess dress is bordered with real pearls dipped in gold. One-of-a-kind and handmade by master craftspeople in some country where they make crafts like this (that I will Google later), you will look like a true Lady of the Evening in this dress. Available in three colors: Electric Midnight, Fusion, and Garrulous."

I do not mean to brag, but I think that I am very good at writing descriptions. Min agrees with me. She says that when she has her fashion house, I can write all the catalogs. Zelda will be the model. I think a job in fashion will go well with my YouTube guru channel.

I also use my computer for PicBomb, although that is a secret because my mother thinks that anyone who is less than twenty-five and is on social media will be instantly killed by stalkers. When I log in, PicBomb tells me that one of my contacts has Joined the Community, which is creepy in a few ways. First, I do not like it when they remind me that they have access to my contacts in my e-mail. That is weird, and I do not know how to shut it off and it makes me feel like they have sent little spybots into my computer that are going to attack me in my sleep. And the second thing I do not like is the way that they refer to PicBomb as a "Community," as if we are Amish or in a cult together or something.

I click on the little person icon and see a photo of a familiar forehead and the name Anna Hernandez, and my heart feels like someone has blown helium into it. Of course I click accept, and I wonder if Anna got a smartphone. No, of course she didn't get a smartphone. She's still probably buying her sneakers at Discount Blowout. I guess she joined on her computer and is taking pics with her flip phone. Still, I kind of like this forehead selfie she posted. She has added a blue filter. I can tell she took the photo in her living room, because in the background I can see the giant fake swordfish on the wall that her father won in a raffle and always tells people he caught off the coast of Cuba. And I can see the clock that is seven minutes fast, so I know that she took the photo at 9:24. But I do not know if she took it in the a.m. or the p.m.

I know everything in that room: the bookcase with the wobbly shelf, the tan carpet that Anna's father always keeps superclean because he never lets anyone wear shoes in the house, the giant flat-screen TV that is constantly playing soccer—even in the morning—and the brown velour recliner that her brother always tries to slip into whenever Mr. Hernandez gets up for a snack. I can even smell that house. It smells like bacon, and like spicy men's deodorant, and like Mrs. Hernandez's dry shampoo, and like some kind of pepper that I never could quite name.

I click the COOL symbol by the photo and wait for something to happen. Nothing does, though. The little red flag tells me that Anna isn't on the site right now. Even if she were, what would I say?

*Hi, how are you? How's Janelle? How Lucinda? How's Leroy? Did you get my messages? I'm good. Not much going on here. Oh, well, Dad kinda lost his job. And there might be a lawsuit. Also, apparently my grandmother is a horrible person? Um, and I have kind of told my new friends that I know Beyoncé and I owe them money that I can't pay back. Oh, and I'm failing history and Desmond is being bullied but . . .*

Ugh. She won't even call or text back when I say that things are *good*.

I close my computer.

Desmond isn't in his room, so I knock on the bathroom door and call softly, "Des?"

"What?" His voice is echoey, bouncing off of the tiles.

"Are you in there using the bathroom, or are you just reading?"

"Reading."

"Can I come in? Just for a minute?"

There is a pause, and then a click as he unlocks the door for me. The bathroom that Desmond and I share is really beautiful, but kind of useless. Our mom had it renovated and decorated before we moved in. She was really into the idea of decorating for a while, until it turned out to be a boring time suck, kind of like making soap. I guess, for some things, it's more fun to think about doing them than it is to actually do them.

Our bathroom has this shower with a huge showerhead that rains down on you, but instead of our old moldy shower curtain that we had in Jersey City, this has a half wall of glass. Not a sliding door, just a glass wall that only goes halfway. It's pretty, but water splashes out of the shower and all over the floor on the daily, which is kind of sad, because that little wall has *one job* and it's too much. There is also a kind of piano bench thingy that my mother used to display rolled-up towels on. She did that for about three weeks, then gave up, because who wants to always be rolling up towels for display? Now we just throw our bathrobes and stuff on the piano bench, usually. But Desmond also likes to read there, and that is what he was doing a moment before I came in. His tablet is facedown on the bench, and I assume he has been reading one of those stories he loves about the mouse and the other mice. I forget what they're called.

At least the bathroom smells nice, because we always use my mom's lemongrass-ginger soap. "What's up?" I ask, leaning against that stupid shower glass. "Are you hungry? You want some chicken?"

"I got something for myself a while ago. Thanks."

"Why don't you go read in your room?"

"I don't like my room." Our mom also had Desmond's

room decorated before we moved in, and for some weird reason, the decorator chose an ocean theme, with lamp bases made of nautical knots and navy and white all over the place, and pictures of sailboats. Which is totally weird, because Desmond has this sort of pathological fear of lobsters and as a result really hates the ocean.

Personally, I like his room and would prefer it to mine, which is brown and blue and has framed maps of New York City on the walls, and a dresser with "Brooklyn" painted on it. It feels kind of random, because I've only lived in New York City for less than a year, and I have never been to Brooklyn, but we were specifically told that the decorator had a "vision" based on having met us for five minutes, and then Mom consulted a colorologist, who predicted the shades that would bring harmony and make us all productive, so I guess I just have to wait for all of that inspiration and good color vibe to sink in. I keep expecting to wake up and like it one day. Everybody else who comes over does.

"This bathroom is the coziest place in the apartment," I say, and it's weirdly true.

"Plus, nobody bothers you when you're in the

bathroom," Desmond agrees.

I am very impressed by this observation and think it is totally mug-worthy, which makes me proud and a little envious at the same time. Desmond scoots over and I sit down next to him on the bench. I put an arm around him and he puts his head on my shoulder. I can smell that he has been stealing my shampoo again, but do not mention it. "Are you worried about tomorrow?"

Desmond shakes his head.

I find it hard to believe that Desmond isn't thinking about Simon, or about Principal Becker, at least. But his mouth is twisted and his nostrils flared, almost like a bull. "Really?"

"Really."

"I would be worried."

Desmond sits up then, and looks right at me. "I'm not you," he says.

"I know that. I mean, like, obvi."

"No—I mean it. Everyone seems to be confused. I'm *me*." My little brother points to his chest. "You're *you*."

I look at him carefully, at his dark eyes that are so serious behind their thick lashes. A lock of straight brown hair is falling over the center of his forehead. He is *serious*; he really wants to *explain this*. But, I mean, obviously: I am me. He is him. This is, like, Tarzan stuff. Me Jane, right?

I don't joke, though. "I understand you, Desmond," I say, and reach for his hand. His fingers feel fragile and small laced through mine.

Small, but not as small as they used to be.

## CHAPTER SEVENTEEN, I THINK?

## In which I wonder, "Who Let in the Rain"

I LOVE WAKING UP on rainy mornings, but only when there is still time to snuggle down in my bed and look out the window. It's fun to watch the water droplets drip into rivers, join other droplets, switch direction, branch off into rivulets, and finally speed down the glass to end in a big, fat splash at the bottom of the sill.

Anna used to always wish that she lived in California, where the weather is sunny and warm. Not me. Not me, because I like to be cozy, and you can never really feel cozy inside unless the weather is bad—too cold or too wet or both—outside.

But ugh, what I do not like is actually getting out of bed.

Desmond is already up and dressed when I get to the

breakfast table. He is watching one of his weird shows. Dad is reading the news on his tablet and gulping coffee, which whirrups down his throat. He is wearing a bathrobe, and his chest hairs poke out of it. Is it strange that some of his chest hairs are gray? His stubble is gray, too. The lines on his face are deep, and I'm realizing that my dad looks . . . old.

I guess Mom is sleeping in. When she was a social worker, she was always up at five thirty. She said that one of the great things about starting her own business is that she can make her own hours. She gets more sleep these days, but she still seems tired.

I kiss Dad on top of his head, and he looks a little surprised, but he smiles at me.

I shake cereal into my bowl, and the three of us sit there in silence. Then I kiss Desmond and head out the door.

Down on the street, the water is coming at me sideways. The city is a dismal place in the rain. Water fills up the potholes and pools in strange ways at the curb so that you are constantly trying to leap over huge puddles while dodging traffic. The taxi drivers actually seem to make a game of trying to splash people—they zoom right up to the edge of the road. Once, I saw this lady get nailed by an absolute tsunami of brown pothole water. And the other thing that happens is that rain always seems to bounce up off the pavement so that your legs are wet by the time you get to where you are going.

To put it philosophically: bad weather is okay, as long as you don't have to go out in it. Because otherwise it's a mess to deal with.

So I am very relieved to get to my grandmother's apartment lobby. Robert is wearing his full-length raincoat today, and a little shower-cap–style protector over his hat. He scowls at my feet as I track rain into the lobby.

"Hi, Robert."

Robert cocks his head slightly, which I think is maybe a kind of a salute. Anyway, I take it as a compliment and head over to the elevator, and who should be stepping out of the mail room but Mr. Johnson!

"Callie!" he says warmly, as if he knows me really well. "Are you on your way up to your grandmother's apartment?"

"Yes." We both step into the elevator, and Mr. Johnson

punches both 19 and 20, which I think is quite gentlemanly. "Did you go for a walk?" I ask. His hair is tousled and damp, and his jacket is speckled with rain.

"Sure did! Every morning, to grab my joe." He holds up a blue paper coffee cup with a white Greek key pattern on it. "Forget all the French press drip pour-over espresso nonsense! For coffee, you can't beat the Greek deli!"

"That's exactly what my dad says, only he says it about bagel sandwiches."

"Wise man." The elevator bings and slows to a stop. There is a pause, almost like the machine is catching its breath, before the door opens and Mr. Johnson steps out into the hallway. "Would you mind taking something up to Hildy for me?"

"Oh, sure." I step out into the hallway, and Mr. Johnson walks down the hallway to apartment 1986.

"I'll just be a minute," he says, ducking inside. "You can come in, if you like."

I kind of half step into the entranceway, leaving the door open behind me. Mr. Johnson crouches down, flipping through the vinyl records on his bottom shelf until he finds the one he is looking for. I take the opportunity to look around the apartment. A framed black-and-white painting is on the wall. It looks like intestines, or squiggles, but when I look more closely, I see that there are human figures mixed in. Some seem to be trapped, others are stacked, some are held by giant hands.

"Keith Haring started as a subway artist," Mr. Johnson says when he sees me looking.

"I think I've seen his stuff."

"A lot of it is iconic. This is for Hildy." He holds an album with five people floating on a red field. They're photographed at odd angles. *Blue Angel* is written across the cover.

I look more closely at the figure on the left. "Is that Cyndi Lauper?"

"This was her first band—Blue Angel."

"I love her."

"Your uncle did, too, according to your grandmother. This is for her. I don't think she realizes that I meant for her to keep it."

I look up at Mr. Johnson. He has a wide, even smile, and I think he is pretty good-looking, even though he is mostly bald, with only short white hair on the sides of his head. His cheeks are pink, probably from being out in the cold rain, and he looks almost like an illustration from a children's book, the kind where the characters have eyes that twinkle. He seems like the kind of person you can really talk to, so I decide to just go for it. "Why is this place so eighties?" I ask him.

He lets out a long, loud laugh. "What's wrong with the eighties?"

"What's wrong with *now*?" I shoot back.

He laughs again. "Lots!"

"Well—lots was wrong with the eighties, too." I don't actually know if this is true, but I'm a little defensive about the present, for some reason. I guess because it's my home, and all.

But Mr. Johnson doesn't get mad. He just says, "That is the truth!" and laughs again. "Well, Callie, I never really meant to have such an extensive collection of memorabilia, to tell you the truth. But I sold my first company in 1983, and I started collecting things. I started with *Star Wars* figures. Once you start collecting, well—sometimes the collection just takes over. Now I deal in 1980s art and collectibles; I've still got a shop downtown. But I like living with all these relics. The phones are easier to use. And I love the music. The new stuff, well—it makes me feel old. Here in my little apartment, I have more energy. It's like I'm the same young man I used to be."

I look around the apartment. There's a phone on the wall, the kind with a curly cord. And a huge box with a tiny screen—I think that's the computer. It's strange, but I can kind of see how this place is like a time machine. Like the Temple of Dendur. When you're there, it's easy to imagine the desert and the Egyptians all around you. Time is such a strange thing. It's so weird to think that maybe this age—the one I am right now—will be something I miss when I'm older. I guess I can't imagine being that different from how I am now—won't most of my thoughts be the same? Won't I still be me?

I hug the album to my chest and say, "I'll get this to her. But I don't think she has a record player."

"She does," Mr. Johnson says. "Or she will—tomorrow. It's being delivered." He gives me a wink and a mustache-y smile that makes me giggle.

Mr. Johnson waits by the door and I call out, "Bye!" just as the elevator door chunks closed again. He's a little weird, but at least I know that he's nice and has good taste in grandmothers.

I swing open my grandmother's front door, and Biddy greets me, winding around my legs (which is *ew* because they are kind of wet and now have cat hair on them) and sputter-meowing.

"Gran?" I call.

"Callie?" she calls from the kitchen, and a moment later she appears, wiping her hands on a decorative dish towel.

I hold up the album and say, "This is from Mr. Johnson."

"Oh." My grandmother takes the album and looks down at it. "That was nice of him." Her voice is faint, though. Like a shadow of a voice.

"You don't want it?"

Her brown eyes snap onto mine. "Larry used to play this all the time when he was in high school." She sighs and looks at me. "We would dance around the apartment."

"Oh."

She looks at the album for a long time then. "I remember when Larry bought this. He used to spend all of his allowance downtown, at the music stores." With a sigh, she places the record on the coffee table, in the exact place where the *Time* magazines were a few days before. Then she walks over to the plaid wing chair beside the couch and sort of sinks onto the cushion. She looks up at the painting of Larry, and my heart starts to pound. It's so uncomfortable to see adults feeling sad. I kind of wish I could change the subject, but I know that won't help. "Do you still miss Uncle Larry?"

"Very much. They say that time heals all wounds, but . . ." Her voice trails off. I try to imagine what it would be like for my parents if I died, or if Desmond did, and then I regret thinking that thought, because if anything happened to Desmond I would never get over it. *Never.*

"It has been interesting, spending time with Earl. His apartment brings up so many memories for me . . ." For a moment, everything is so silent that I hear the hum of the refrigerator from the kitchen. Biddy has perched herself in a windowsill, and is looking down at the wet weather with cat disapproval. Only one floor lamp is lit, and it's dim and dreamlike in the living room.

"Sometimes, I wish I could go back in time. I wish

things could be the way they were," my grandmother says at last.

"Back when you and Larry would dance around the house?"

"Back before things got . . . complicated." She casts her eyes up to the painting. "That's how I like to remember him—the way he was in that self-portrait."

I stare at it for a moment. I've never really looked at that painting closely before. It was just always there. "Who's the other guy?" I ask.

Grandma Hildy looks confused. "What other guy?"

"The other guy in the painting."

"It's a self-portrait. Larry is looking in a mirror."

I cock my head, but I'm pretty sure I'm right. "It's not a mirror."

Grandma Hildy insists, though. "You see the way his hand is pressed up against the fingertips in his reflection?"

"It's a window." I walk over to the painting and squint at it, but I'm sure. The vantage point is over a man's shoulder. He is wearing a navy blue jacket. Through the window and viewed from the front, Larry is also wearing a navy blue jacket. But Larry's shirt is white, and the strip of collar visible above the other man's jacket is pale blue. And there's more. "Their hair isn't the same." I point out the slightly different shades of brown. "And there's this little bit of cuff on the sleeve; see how it's different from Larry's? It's meant to look like a self-portrait, but he's really looking at someone else. Their fingers are almost touching, just separated by the glass."

My grandmother is staring, and I'm feeling pretty proud of myself, and like my week at the museums has really paid off. Slowly, slowly, she gets to her feet and walks over to the buffet. She picks up the photo I found in my bag—the one of Larry and my dad and their friend. "It's Stephen," Grandma Hildy whispers. And then she stares up at the painting some more. "He's looking at Stephen."

I walk over and stand by her elbow. I can see that she's probably right. Stephen is wearing a navy blazer in the picture—and a blue shirt. "Hey, that's cool!" I say, but my grandmother does not look like it's cool. She's gone pale. "Are you okay?"

"I'm fine," she whispers.

"Are you—are you sure?"

In the kitchen, the phone begins to ring. "I should get that," Grandma Hildy says. "I'm fine, Callie. I'm—thank you." She gives me a quick hug.

"Oh, you're welcome."

She smiles at me, and even though her eyes are sad, it doesn't seem like a fake smile. It seems real.

"Bye," I call as she hurries off to the answer the phone.

I take one last look at my uncle's painting, at his expression, which is happy and hopeful and dreamy. He looks a little like Grandma Hildy did the other day, when she was thinking about Mr. Johnson.

I wonder what it means.

## CHAPTER EIGHTEEN

# Frick

Cassius is waiting for me on Seventieth Street in front of the Frick Collection. He is wearing this crazy rain poncho that is kind of pulled tight around his head, so that only his face is sticking out beneath a small brim. He looks like he is ready to go camping in the woods as the rain streams down the silver plastic. He is also wearing sunglasses.

"You look like one of those silver balloons they have in balloon bouquets," I tell him. "You should see yourself."

"I guess I'm lucky that I can't." He smiles, and I feel the tight ball of yarn that has been wound up inside my chest all morning start to unravel. A droplet of water is dripping from the tip of Cassius's nose, just hanging out there, and I don't even say anything. I don't care about it. I'm just so glad he's here. Cassius is wet and poorly dressed, but I sort of like that about him. He doesn't care about impressing me, and I know I'm not impressing him, because I'm not even trying.

Yes, I am skipping school again. I have realized that it will actually just be easier to skip the rest of the week. Then I can maybe just tell Zelda that I'm too sick to go to the concert and I'll find a way to get her the money later. The only problem is that homework is piling up. But then, I guess no plan is perfect.

We walk inside together and stand for a moment, dripping onto the marble.

There's just something about the Frick.

I mean, it used to be someone's house! People used to live here! That seems both amazing and totally messed up to me. Kind of like the royal family in England, or the Kardashians—like, it's really cool that those guys get to wear jewels and crazy fashions and travel all over the world and stuff. Cool for *them*. But why are *they* so special? Like, what have any of them ever done except be born to the right people? Is it fair that *the Kardashians* exist while Anna has to shop at Discount Blowout?

These are the kinds of deep thoughts that one can have at the Frick, which is easily one of the most beautiful museums in the world. I think it's nice that the family gave it away along with the art in it so that normal people such as myself can come in and take a look around without having to get a job as a scullery maid.

The entrance hall is this gorgeous room with all of these curlicue marble things at the top of the walls, near the ceiling. It leads straight down to the garden court, which is an open area with a marble fountain and a massive curved skylight. I love that court—it would be the perfect place to have a swanky party or commit a murder or something. Even though the day is gray, dim light gleams at the end of the hall, and I can see the edge of some giant palm frond. We stop at the smooth brown desk on the right and show our passes to the man with the comb-over behind the counter. He has a bit of a cold and snuffles into a handkerchief as he gives us the entry stickers. Then we drop off our wet stuff at the cloak room, and my umbrella goes into a plastic bag, where it will be safe.

I ask if we can just head to the courtyard for a minute, and Cassius says sure. Neither of us is here to see anything in particular, so we're not really in a hurry. When we get there, I stand by the fountain and look at the neatly manicured plants all around me. Then I take a deep breath. The air is sweet, but not like Bath and Body Works perfume-sweet. This is probably some of the best air in Manhattan. They should bottle it and sell it in the gift shop, so that people could inhale it when they're having a stressful day or if they get a lungful of exhaust fumes or a noseful of body odor on the bus.

"What are you doing?" Cassius asks.

"Just breathing." I take another deep inhale. Then I let it out.

Cassius takes a deep breath, too. "Are we meditating?"

"Can't a girl just breathe without it being a thing?"

"Okay." Cassius and I breathe some more, and he doesn't say anything else, which is totally the nicest thing he could do. So we just stand there breathing like a couple of breathing lunatics, and the yarn ball in my stomach unspools and unspools until it is just thread. This is even better than being on the roof of my school because I do not have to worry that I will be late for class or that a meteor will drop on me from outer space while my eyes are closed, and also because Cassius is with me.

I think maybe I should write to Althea about this.

When we are done breathing, we head to the Oval Room, which is in the shape of an oval, so that is quite a coincidence. The paintings are all these tall portraits by this Whistler guy, and they are lovely. These are not the kinds of paintings that are my favorite to look at, but if I could paint, I would want to paint like that, because if I could paint like that I would know that I was a good painter.

Cassius does his usual weird staring thing, where he tilts his head way back and leans in way forward to inspect some detail in the background of the painting—maybe the wallpaper or the hem of the woman's dress. I notice a security guard looking at him strangely, which I must say does not surprise me anymore.

We make our way through the rooms. I think my favorite is the Fragonard room because the art is huge and it is all of these fancy ladies frolicking around in meadows, and it is the easiest room to imagine as my own, because it has this amazingly huge mirror with a gold frame that I could totally see in my room.

"Fragonard," I say out loud. It is very fun to say *Frag-onard*, so I say it again. "Frag . . . o . . . nard."

Cassius laughs. "It's French."

"Oh. Frag-*uh*-narrrrrrrrrrrrcchhh?" I ask with a kind of a choking gurgling sound. I don't speak French, but that is how French sounds to me, and I must be somewhat right because Cassius says, "Yes, exactly," but he is laughing, so it is a bit hard to tell if my pronunciation was really perfect.

We make our way into this vestibule, and I start to head toward the staircase, but while I take the first step, Cassius trips and sprawls flat on his face. His fall echoes crazily, bouncing off the marble floor, walls, stairs.

"Are you okay?" I ask as Cassius lets out a string of curses. He rolls over and sits up, holding his hands over his nose. When he takes them away, a small trickle of blood is coming out of his right nostril.

"I'm fine," he says.

"You're bleeding!" I reach for his elbow to try to help him up, but he jerks it away.

"I'm *fine*." Cassius stumbles to his feet unsteadily and knocks over a freestanding plaque with information about an ancient bowl. The plaque clatters, and I swear that it is so loud that it sounds like someone just shot a wooden ship out of a cannon on top of a volcano. A security guard comes running over.

"We're fine! It's fine!" I pick up the plaque.

"Please don't touch the plaque, miss," the guard says, so I drop it again, which was maybe not the best move because it crashes to the floor and the plaque breaks off of the stand. "Oh, crap!"

"I'm sorry." Cassius takes a deep breath, but his voice is still shaking. "I tripped on the steps here and I knocked over the plaque."

"It was an accident," I put in.

"I didn't see it," Cassius says. He sounds furious and embarrassed, and I don't blame him. "You should consider adding some bright tape to these steps."

"Tape?" the guard repeats.

"It's dangerous for people with a vision impairment," Cassius goes on.

"Do people with vision impairments visit art museums?" I ask.

"I'm telling you that *I* have a vision impairment, and

the light's so dim that I had trouble seeing the low step."

"I see," the guard replies. "Are you all right?"

"Yes," but Cassius sounds like, *No, you jerk, obviously.*

"There are a lot of rare pieces of China and enamel . . ." the guard begins.

"Are you concerned that I might knock them over?" Cassius demands.

The guard doesn't say anything.

"I'll be very careful." Cassius's voice is slow and deliberate. Then, bitter: "My friend will keep an eye out." And here, he looks at me, so of course I back him up.

"I'll help him," and I grab Cassius's hand, and the guard nods like that is okay and then goes away, thank goodness.

Once she's gone, we turn and start up the steps. We go slowly. I hold Cassius's arm. "Why did you say that?" I whisper.

"Because it's true." Cassius does not whisper.

"No, it isn't."

Cassius stops on the stairs, but he does not look at me. "I have Best disease," he says slowly. "The center of my vision has a big blot on it. That's why I look at everything like this." And then he tilts his head back crazily and looks at me with his nostrils again. I can see that there is still a small smudge of red beneath his right nostril, but think, *I can't wipe that for him without looking like I'm trying to pick his nose,* and then . . .

And then . . .

Well, I don't really know what to do. I am standing here, looking up Cassius's nose, and as usual, my mind veers suddenly and I am thinking about this singer, Michael Jackson.

Once, my mom told a story. She said that when Michael Jackson died, they found all of these drugs in his body. And it was really strange, because her whole life, she had just thought that Michael Jackson was a weirdo. Like, he bought the bones of the Elephant Man and had a best friend who was a chimpanzee and stuff like that. "I thought he was crazy," Mom told me, "but he was really just on drugs. SO DON'T DO DRUGS." That was the moral of that story.

But right now, I am thinking about how my mom thought that Michael Jackson was crazy, but he was really sick with drugs. And I thought that Cassius was . . . I don't know, kinda weird and not good with people, but really he has some disease that makes him . . . not see very well?

And before I know what's happening, I just start crying. Like, tears are streaming down my face until it's as wet as it was when I was out in the rain, and Cassius is just standing there, and I realize that OHMYGOD he doesn't even know I'm crying because he can't see me! I let out a big sniffle.

"Are you crying?" Cassius asks.

"Yes."

"Why? *You're* not going blind."

"*What?*" My voice is screechy, and the stairway is superechoey, so I lower the volume. "Now you're going *blind*?"

"Isn't that why you're crying?"

I huff, "I *was* crying because you are *vision impaired*! I didn't know you were going *blind*, too!"

Cassius shakes his head. "You are a trip, Callie."

"Is it getting *worse*? You're going to go *blind*-blind? Like completely?" I'm pleading with him now, but I don't know what I expect him to say. My hand is still on his arm, and he puts his fingers over mine. Then he gently guides me back down the stairs and for a minute my eyes are so watery that I can hardly see and I think, *Oh it's the blind leading the blind,* but I do not say that because I am not completely an insensitive jerk.

At least, not out loud.

Down the hallway, and then we are back in the garden court, and I take a few deep breaths until I feel sort of hollowed out, like a decorative Halloween gourd. We sit on the lip of the fountain. We just breathe awhile, but it's not as nice as it was before.

"When I found out that I had Best disease," Cassius says finally, "and that I was going to go blind, I told my parents that I didn't want to waste any more time in school. I needed to see things. I needed to see them *now*, while I could. So we agreed that as long as I could still get around, I could go do what I wanted, and we would find a way to make it into schoolwork." He reaches out and strokes a leaf with a fingertip. "I couldn't stand being in school, and having everyone . . . you know."

"How do you . . ." I taste the salt as a tear trickles into the corner of my mouth. "How do you read?"

"I listen, mostly. Audiobooks."

I pause and then—

"Why am *I* crying?" I can't stop. I'm trying and I really can't. "Why aren't you crying? What's wrong with you? *You should be crying!*"

"I guess I've had more time to get used to it. And mostly, I just feel really lucky that I can still see. You know, for the most part."

And this makes me cry harder, but more quietly, at least. I pull a small mirror out of my messenger bag. "Ugh," I say, brushing away my tears. I look like a complete hag—my face is all splotchy and my eyes are red and I have, like, bags under them. "You're so lucky you can't see me right now."

Cassius's face wrinkles into a smile. "You always find a bright side, Callie."

Cassius puts an arm around my shoulder, and I lean my head against his chest. I inhale the sweet smell of the garden mixed with the sweet smell of Cassius. I don't know if it's his hair or his deodorant, or what, but he smells really good. I close my eyes and I just concentrate on those smells.

"Are you okay?" Cassius asks after a while.

"Yes."

Cassius starts to shift, like maybe he wants to get up, and so I open my eyes and look up at him. "Can we stay here? Just a little longer?"

He looks down at me from his curious angle. "Sure."

We sit there for a while. Every now and then, a single person or a couple will walk into the courtyard, but none of them linger.

My cheek is against his shoulder. He is wearing an olive green T-shirt, and it must be one of those ridiculously expensive ones, because it's soft as a pillowcase. I can feel his collarbone against my ear, and I can hear his heart beating. It's an interesting thing, that everyone has a heart. It just pulses away, and you never really pay any attention to it.

Except when it's breaking, of course.

## CHAPTER NINETEEN

# In which . . . enlightenmentation

"NOW, IF YOU WILL slowly open your eyes, you should feel your body filled with light and energy . . ." Tinkly music and the sound of ocean waves roll from a small speaker.

The man in the big khaki overcoat lets out a loud snore, but the old lady in the pink suit opens her eyes and blinks. She has a sweet smile, and I really like how she matched her lipstick to her handbag. "Oh, that feels wonderful!" she says in a German accent, so it sounds like "vonnder-vul!" She's so cute; I could just put her into my pocket.

"Feel the positive energy . . ." my mother is saying.

"Vonnderful!"

The man snores again. My mother tries to ignore him, but the German lady gives him a poke. "Vake up, you!"

He does not move, and from the smell coming off of

him, I think he might not wake up for a while. He smells like he just came from Beertown. Like maybe he went swimming in the Beer Pool there and then took a Beer Shower. And then rode to Manhattan in a Beer Cab . . . while drinking a beer.

"Take a deep breath in through your nose . . ." My mother inhales deeply, and then realizes what a mistake this is, since she is sitting next to Beer Guy. She coughs, and the German lady pounds her on the back. "Take a . . . cleansing . . . (cough, cough) breath through your mouth . . ."

Let me just tell you one thing: this is not the worst workshop I've seen my mom give.

In addition to selling soap, once a month my mom runs a meditation workshop at the local library. Did you know that there were libraries in Manhattan? Well, neither does anybody else, which is one of the reasons that nobody ever comes to these things.

But my mother just says that it makes her feel good to help people relax and direct their energy. She also volunteers helping out-of-work people with their résumés. It's kind of like the social work she used to do, except that this pays nothing, which is even less than she used to earn.

At the end of the session, Beer Guy is still asleep, but the old woman gives my mother a hug. "Zat vas vonnderful! Vonnderful!"

My mother sighs happily as she watches the old woman leave. "Sometimes, I really feel like I'm making a difference," she says, and I think about how great my mom is at positive thinking. Really, she's a natural.

We walk up Fifth Avenue, and my mother stops to sigh over a dress in the Saks window. It's very pretty, and I think it would look great on my mother, and I say so.

"When would I wear a dress like that?"

"You could just wear it around the apartment," I suggest. "Or to a Pie Soiree, or something."

"I don't think I'll be having another Pie Soiree," Mom says. Her voice is sad, but it's sad in the way it is when you're just saying something that you know is true.

"Why not? I thought you said that the last one went well."

Mom shrugs. "Well, a lot of those people were from the fund, so I don't think we'll be seeing them again any time soon. They weren't as great as I thought they were, anyway." A few steps away a homeless man sits near the curb. Before him is a can that reads, "Homeless veteran. Please help!"

Mom reaches into her handbag for her wallet.

"Thank you," the man says as she drops a five-dollar bill into the can. Then she looks through the file she is holding and pulls out a piece of paper. "Here's a list of resources—shelters, meal programs, stuff like that."

The man looks surprised. "You a social worker, or something?"

"Used to be."

He folds up the paper and tucks it into a pocket. "God bless you." He sounds really sincere, and for a moment I get this weird feeling, like maybe he's a holy man or something, dressed up in dirty clothes to try to trick us into being kind. But a moment later, I realize that, no—he's just a regular poor dude. Still, that nice feeling stays on me. My mom thanks him for the blessing, and we walk on.

"Do you ever miss working at Pooh Corner?" That's what we called the place where she used to work, which was really called Unity House, and was on the corner of Wynne and Pugh Street. When I was a kid, I thought it was "Winnie the Pooh" instead of Wynne and Pugh. Pooh Corner.

"I do. I thought it would be fun to start my own business and be my own boss. But it turns out that making soap and running a business is just as much work as being a social worker, and sometimes it feels a little . . ."

"Pointless?"

She laughs. "Yeah."

"Do you ever think about going back?"

My mom keeps walking. She is staring straight ahead. "Sometimes it's not that easy."

I think about Grandma Hildy, and how she wishes she could go back and do things differently.

"Why was Grandpa Constantine so mad at Uncle Larry?" I ask. My mom and I are walking side by side, and I notice that our strides are the same length. We are almost the same height now, which is strange.

She lets out a sigh. "Your grandfather was an old-fashioned man, Callie. He had old-fashioned beliefs. And those were different times. So he forbade anyone in the family to have contact with Larry. Honestly, I don't know if your grandmother ever got over it when he died."

I feel like something has lodged in my heart—like a stone, or an arrow, maybe. "But why would she agree to that?"

"Everything was so different then. A lot of people really thought that being gay was a sin, and that people could choose not to be gay."

"But Uncle Larry was her son!"

"Yes, but she thought he was going through a phase. She thought that it would pass. Constantine made her choose, and she chose him. But I think she really believed that either Constantine or Larry would come around after a while. I don't think she ever expected Larry to die so soon . . . None of us did."

"And dad? He didn't talk to his *own brother*?"

My mother stops and faces me. Her brown eyes are like warm chocolate. "Callie—why do you think your father was written out of the will?"

And just like that, the whole situation comes crashing down on me, squashing me flat. It is like the sky has fallen on me.

My dad refused to listen to my grandfather. My

grandfather punished him for it.

"Your father always supported Larry. He was there at the end, even though it cost him . . ." I am still crushed beneath the sky, but I can hear my mother's voice. "Your dad is a loyal man, Callie. He always does what he thinks is right, even when it's hard. He kept working for the family business even after Constantine refused to go to Larry's funeral—"

"*What?* He didn't go to the *funeral*?"

"No. Stephen was going to be there, so he didn't go."

"Stephen." I remember the man in the photo. "Uncle Larry's friend?"

"His boyfriend."

His boyfriend? Suddenly, the painting in my grandmother's apartment makes sense. Perfect sense. "Did Grandma Hildy go to the funeral?"

"Yes."

I am so relieved that the sidewalk goes a little blurry. I'm not sure why that is important to me, but it is. My mother reaches for my arm, because I am about to step off the curb and into the traffic because, apparently, my brains were squashed out of my head when the sky fell on me.

My mother's eyes are teary. Her warm hand is still on my arm, and suddenly I am having this weird thought that my mother used to be *my* age, and even Desmond's age.

I wonder if Desmond and I will be different when we grow up, or if we will just still have the same kinds of thoughts and worries that we have right now. Like, will we still be kids, kinda, just in these weird old wrinkly bodies? Looking at my mother, I am almost positive that I am seeing young her—Little Mom, who is just trying to make the best of things. "Callie, we're having a tough moment right now," she says after a while, and I know she is talking about my dad's job and the money situation and all of that. "But things will get better. They always do."

I know she's right. This world and everything in it, it's all just swirling around us and you can't even hang on to anything, because everything is always changing.

My mother closes her eyes again and breathes, just breathes in and out for a moment, and I feel her getting stronger as the bad feelings pass away, kind of like clouds passing across the sky. She looks up at me. "That's why we have to try to live without regrets," she says to me. Then she turns toward traffic that has been rushing by us, and faces the people on their cell phones, the people hiding behind sunglasses, just trying to get home, the taxis and the hissing bus on the corner. "LIVE WITHOUT REGRETS!" she shouts.

Nobody looks up.

The light changes, and we cross the street, and we disappear into this big swirling ever-changing cloud of people—just trying to get home now, like everybody else.

## CHAPTER TWENTY

# In which our heroine makes a decision

ONCE WE GET HOME, I volunteer to go pick up Desmond at improv class. On the way there, I stop to pick up a big soft pretzel and I put mustard over the whole thing, just like Desmond likes it.

I can't wait to see him, and hear about his day with Simon Yee. I'll bet it was much better, now that there's no lunch bag to worry about!

Improv class is in the basement of his school, but when I get there I don't see Desmond in the group of kids, who have, apparently, turned themselves into a living machine. They are pumping their arms and twisting their bodies, and making whirs and clangs and gongs, and it looks like fun, but Desmond is sitting by himself with his back against the wall, not even looking at the other kids. The teacher, Ms. Taymor, waves at me enthusiastically, and then points to Desmond and shakes her head, then makes some intricate hand gestures that seem to mean *I don't know what's wrong*, so I walk over to him and sit down beside him on the floor.

"What happened?" I whisper, looking up and down his arms for bruises. "Did Simon—"

"Simon didn't say anything to me today," Desmond says. "Not a word."

"Well—that's great." I hand him the big, fat pretzel, and he smiles a little.

"You're so nice to me, Callie." His eyes fill with tears, and I just want to hug him. He takes a bite of the pretzel.

The group in front is still whirring and gonging, and Ms. Taymor shakes her black curls and shouts, "Take it to a TEN!" and the whirring and gonging gets louder and crazier.

Desmond just chews his pretzel and I can tell that he is not even seeing this crazy machine in front of us.

"If Simon left you alone then why are you—"

"He left me alone, but he started picking on Zephyr. He said he was a fat dummy."

"*What?*" Now I'm mad. Zephyr is basically the nicest kid in the world. Okay, second nicest. "Zephyr's barely even chubby! Why would he do that?"

"Take it to a ONE!" Ms. Taymor shouts, and the machine quiets down, and the movements get smaller.

The room has grown almost silent, so Desmond whispers, "Because Simon Yee is a rampallian."

"Desmond, I'm sure he's a mammal."

"That means a horrible person, Callie."

"Oh. Well at least he's not bothering *you*—"

"What difference does it make? It bothers *me* when my friends get picked on," Desmond says, and the words hit me like a slap.

Ms. Taymor waves her arm at the group, flapping the long, loose sleeve of her tunic. "Pause, everyone! Pause button! Pause!" Then she turns to me and Desmond. "Would you please—" She gestures wildly with her hands, somehow communicating that we should be quieter. "It's so hard for the actors—"

"This is not a professional environment," says one little girl with braids.

"Sorry, guys," I announce to the group of seven- and

eight-year-olds. "I think we're going to—" And I gesture to Ms. Taymor to indicate that Desmond and I are leaving. I guess I'm just trying to communicate in her language. She nods and then gestures that she hopes Desmond feels better, and that maybe we should check his temperature to make sure he doesn't have a fever, and then I nod, and she turns back to the machine and cries, "RESUME!" and it all starts back up again.

I grab Desmond's backpack for him, since he's busy with the pretzel, and we trudge up the stairs.

"That's what I've been saying," Desmond tells me in the stairwell. "Simon Yee is awful. It's just how he is . . ."

"I really thought he would stop after you got rid of the lunch bag."

Desmond sighs. "It's not about the lunch bag," he says.

"Well, maybe it's a little about the lunch bag."

Desmond looks at me, his dark eyes serious beneath his floppy bangs. "No," he says simply. "It's not."

For some reason, I am still thinking about Desmond and Simon Yee and the lunch bag after dinner, when I am in my room, supposedly doing my history homework, ha, ha.

I am considering calling Min. But what would Min do? Freak out, maybe, and then try to get into a poorly spelled Twitter war with Simon Yee.

What about Zelda? She wouldn't even understand why I'm butting into my brother's problems. She has three older brothers, but they're all either off at college or long out of it, and it's basically like they live on a distant planet—one without phones to call home.

The person I want to call is Anna. Not just because Anna knows Desmond better than Min or Zelda do, but because I know Anna will say what I need someone to say. She will be *mad*. She will want revenge. Nobody messes with anybody around Anna. "Somebody needs to go to beat-down school," she would say.

Look, I do not believe in physical violence. Of course, I also do not believe in Santa Claus, but that does not stop me from jumping out of bed on Christmas morning.

I am not saying that I am planning to beat up Simon Yee! I am only saying that I wish I knew someone who would do it for me. Except that I kind of want the satisfaction of dealing with Simon myself.

Because something is dawning on me. I feel like

someone just set my hair on fire! Literally! Except not literally, because then my head would be on fire, but you know what I mean!

Desmond was right: it's not about the lunch bag. It's *never* about the lunch bag.

It's about being a bully.

Even though I tried to help Desmond, I didn't help him. I didn't help him *be Desmond*—I tried to just tell him to act like someone else, to get a different lunch bag, to blend in, to pretend . . .

I thought I was Keeping It Positive! But, really, I just didn't stick up for him. The same way I didn't stick up for Anna.

I think about my dad, and how he stood up for his brother, even though it cost him. All he wanted was for Uncle Larry to be able to be himself.

I start dialing the phone before I realize what I'm doing. But, as usual, I have to leave a message. "Hey. Hey, Anna. You know, I've been thinking. About the pie party. My mom was kind of weird that day. I think it was basically temporary insanity. But she's better now. Anyway, that's not the point. The point is that I should have stood up for you. I'm better now, too. I just, uh . . . I wanted you to know that. I miss you."

I click off, and it is amazing how much better I feel. I feel relaxed, and calm. Like, maybe this is what meditation is supposed to feel like.

"Wow, this is so Zen," I murmur. Just then, the phone buzzes in my hand and I am so surprised that I scream and throw it across the room.

When I scramble off my bed and pick the phone out of the garbage can it landed in, I see that the person calling is Anna. My heart freaks out, and for a moment, I consider throwing the phone away again. No. God! What is my problem? Anna is my *friend*! And she is finally calling back!

"Hello?"

"Hey—Callie. It's Anna."

"I know. I know! Hi!"

"Hi."

"Hi!"

She laughs softly. "Hi. Again."

"I'm so glad to hear from you!"

"Yeah. I'm sorry I haven't called . . . I just got your

message." She blows out a breath, and I can imagine her bangs fluttering the way they do when she does that.

"Yeah . . ." Anna's voice sounds different. She sounds cautious. This is the first time it really hits me that I hurt her feelings. The last time I saw Anna, we were saying good-bye on the pavement in front of my apartment building. She gave me this weak little hug and sort of looked behind me, to where the tiny blue lights glowed on a huge silver-and-teal holiday wreath, illuminating the white wall in the lobby. "Thanks for having me at your pie party," she said.

"Thanks for coming."

And then her dad pulled up in his van, and Ivan opened the door for Anna. She glanced at him, and said, "You sure are lucky, Callie." The door closed, and the van pulled away.

I didn't want her to leave.

"You were waiting for me to apologize," I say now.

"I guess so. I guess . . . I thought you had changed." She's silent for a moment. "I'm glad the insanity was temporary."

"Well—I didn't say it was *over*."

Anna laughs.

"So—so what's going on?"

So Anna tells me all about what's going on with our friends. How Leroy and Janelle were a couple for a while, and it almost broke Jannie's heart because of course she's had a crush on him since sixth grade. And how Minti wants everyone to use his real name—Mintesinot—now, but everyone keeps forgetting and calling him Minti. And how the science teacher got fired last month, and the substitute has a weird smell.

And I tell Anna about Desmond and Simon Yee, and of course she is furious on my brother's behalf. It feels so good to have someone listen for a while. But it turns out that I don't really need her help, after all. I already know what I'm going to do.

I'm going to walk my brother to school tomorrow morning.

By the time we get off the phone, it's late, and I don't feel like dealing with my history homework. But that's okay, because I'm not going to school tomorrow, anyway. I'll just call in another excuse and then make a fresh start on Monday.

My phone buzzes; it's a text from Zelda: *Are you coming tomorrow?* and I cringe. Uggh. I don't even dare to text her back. I don't have her money. I can't face her. I can't deal with everything all at once.

But I *can* face Simon Yee.

## CHAPTER FIVE THOUSAND, FOUR HUNDRED, AND SEVENTY-SIX, OR THAT'S WHAT IT FEELS LIKE

## In which someone goes to beat-down school

"THAT'S HIM," DESMOND SAYS, although I already know what Simon Yee looks like. He looks like a preppy kid in a school uniform, that's what he looks like. He wears his clothes like a rich kid. I can't explain it, but they look cleaner, and their skin is better, and their hair is more . . . I don't know . . . *glossy*. Simon Yee looks like he spends his spare time posing for Ralph Lauren Kids ads. And he's got that Ralph Lauren Kids model look on his face—smug, and bored, and *oooooh, I just want to smack him*. But I will not. I will restrain myself because I am going to be mature.

The whole block is closed to traffic for the half hour before and after school, and the kids run wild all over the street, as if it's a normal playground. Older kids lounge close to the buildings, but younger ones are screaming, jumping rope, playing tag, gossiping, just like they would in any suburb or small town or city. It's funny how some of them—like Simon—look like rich kids, while some of them look regular and you would not know that they were rich as heck except that they, obviously, go to this school, which costs as much as college and I am not even exaggerating.

"You wait here," I say to Desmond, depositing him near the gate.

"Just be careful, Callie," Desmond warns. "He's dangerous."

"Des, I think I can handle a third grader."

Desmond shrugs, like okay, but he doesn't seem very sure and I force myself to try very hard to not be annoyed that my little brother does not have faith in me.

I—very, very calmly because I am being mature—walk over to Simon. He is outside of the gate, standing near a tree, chatting with a couple of other bored-looking kids. They're all short. I'm a head taller than they are. *I could crush you*, I think, looking at Simon.

"Simon, may I please speak to you?" I say very maturely.

Simon looks me up and down. "Sorry, I don't have any spare change."

One of his little friends says, "Oooooo," and the other one says, "*Burn.*"

I turn on them. "What are you two—his minions? Get out of here, turd-brains!" I shout, and while I realize that this may not have been a very mature thing to say, it is effective, because the two henchmen scurry off.

Simon narrows his eyes at me. "What's the deal—Desmond had to send his fat sister in to solve his problems for him?"

"*What?*" I am not even fat, but my face burns. "Listen, you little dung beetle," I say. "You'd better leave my brother alone. And you'd better leave *all of the kids in this class alone.*"

"Or what?"

"Or I'll call your parents."

"Like they'd care."

"Is that it?" A little drop of sympathy oozes into my heart. "Is that why you're so angry? Your parents don't care about you?"

Simon looks like he wants to kill me, and I know I'm right. I'm right! And suddenly, I feel sorry for Simon Yee, and I am also proud of myself for figuring this out, and I realize that I really *am* incredibly mature! I think of my mom's words, "I like to know that I'm helping people," and I think, *Yes. Yes—I know how you feel, Mom!* Poor Simon. He's been lashing out at people because he is suffering. I reach out to touch him on the shoulder and say, "Simon, you don't have to hurt people to get atten—"

But my words are cut off because SIMON KICKS ME IN THE SHIN!

"Ow, you little jerk!" And I reach out to steady myself on the tree because I'm hopping on one foot. And then Simon starts fake-crying and wailing and holding his shoulder, and I'm all, "What are you doing?" and that's when a teacher rushes over to Simon, saying, "What's wrong? What's wrong?" and Simon just points at me and before I know it, I am being escorted to the principal's office.

ME!

"I told you he was dangerous!" Desmond calls.

"*He* is the one who kicked *me*," I say to the woman with the whistle on a lanyard around her neck, who is dragging me down the hall by my arm.

"Save it," the gym teacher says. "I don't listen to bullies."

What????????????

Me—a bully. Yes, she said that!!

So she forces me into a chair outside Mr. Becker's office and then goes in to talk to him. I hear raised voices. This is not going well.

"What happened?" Only half of Mrs. Lewis's head—snow white hair and dark brown forehead—shows over the counter.

"Simon Yee kicked me in the shin."

"Did you kick him back?"

"No!"

"Too bad." The bell rings, and I slump in my chair a little. I'm going to be late to meet Cassius.

"Don't you need to call your school?" The question floats up at me over the counter, and I swear that it takes me a little while to understand what Mrs. Lewis is even asking. It's like I don't think of myself as someone who even *goes* to school anymore. "Haverton, if I remember?"

"Oh—uh . . ." I'm about to say, "No, thanks; I'll just text them from my mom's phone," but then realize that this will seem suspicious, so I say, "Sure. Um. Thank you."

Mrs. Lewis stands up and crosses over to the landline on the counter. "I'll call Roberta for you," she says, and I realize that she means Mrs. Palmer, our school secretary.

"I have the number on my phone—" I say, pulling it out, but Mrs. Lewis just smiles and dials and I realize that she thinks I'm going to pretend to call the school and not really do it, which is, of course, what I *was* going to do, but I am still impressed that she figured it out.

"Hello, Roberta? It's Opal. Yes, I believe I have one of your students here. Mmmm-hmm. Callie Vitalis. Yes, she will be in today, she's just got a meeting with Mr. Becker. Unh-hunh. Right. I'll remind her. Okay, thank you. And I'll see you Thursday? All right, great. Okay, have a great day." Mrs. Lewis hangs up. "She said to remind you that placement testing is today, beginning at nine fifteen."

"Placement testing?!" A dim memory of Zelda stressing out floats through my mind. Ohmygosh, I forgot! This day is getting worse and worse. Now I really do have to get to school—

At that moment, Mr. Becker's door opens, and the gym teacher storms out, glaring.

Mr. Becker's voice drifts over to me. "Please come in, Ms. Vitalis."

Mrs. Lewis lifts her eyebrows and drops back into her chair, and I realize something very important at that moment, which is that Mrs. Lewis has everyone's number and could probably rule the world if the world were a different place.

"Ms. Vitalis, please take a seat." Mr. Becker's elbows are on his desk, and he is holding a pencil perfectly balanced between two fingertips. Somehow, this manages to make him seem like a cartoon villain. "It seems that you have decided to take things into your own hands—"

"I never even touched him! I just wanted to talk to him!"

"Why do members of your family feel the need to antagonize others?"

"He kicked me in the shin!"

"Ms. Vitalis, I'm forced to call your parents about this incident."

"Fine. Call them."

"And I'm not sure that we can continue to offer your brother a place in this school—"

"What?! You're kicking out *Desmond*?!"

"I'm saying that unless I get a satisfactory response from your parents—"

"Listen." I stand up because I have had just about enough of this bull. "Simon Yee is a bully. A clean, cute, adorable bully! This happened because you didn't speak up for Desmond when he needed you! You made him get rid of his *lunch bag*! Well, there is nothing wrong with Desmond's *lunch bag* and there is nothing wrong with *Desmond*! So get your head together, Mr. Becker!" And just like that, I turn and storm out, and I hear Mr. Becker shouting, "Come back here, young lady, I am not done with you!" but I am too busy stomping away and CAUSING DRAMA BEFORE TEN A.M., but as I pass Mrs. Lewis's desk, I see that she is clapping. She's not making any noise, but she is clapping and she is smiling at me, and I stop for just a second, and I smile, too.

"You'd better hurry up," Mrs. Lewis says, glancing at the clock on the wall above my head. It's 8:58. I've got seventeen minutes to get ten blocks uptown—to my so-called school.

I'm going to have to run.

## CHAPTER TWENTY-TWO

## In which our heroine learns to prioritize

IT IS NOT EASY to text and run at the same time, especially in Manhattan, where running down the street is a lot like playing a video game, only one where the obstacles are real, actual human beings and cars and garbage and stuff. I am trying to text Cassius and it is not working.

Cargh . . .

Mah . . .

I feel like Min.

I crash into a man coming out of Le Pain Quotidien on Madison and Eighty-Fourth. "Hey!" he shouts as high-class French iced coffee spills all over his shirt. Luckily, it's a Life Is Good, so it kind of deserves to be spilled on, as they are one of my biggest future competitors in the inspirational mug and T-shirt business.

"Sorry!" I shout over my shoulder as he screams some really creative vocabulary in my direction.

I dart across the street, narrowly dodging a taxi, and leap over three small dogs in a cluster being walked by a dude on a unicycle. (What? This isn't Brooklyn!) My watch says 9:06. I pour on the speed.

"Slow down!" An old man shakes a cane in my direction, but I wave at him anyway, because he's wearing a cute little *Newsies* cap and I love adorable old people.

I pass the dry cleaner's, the weird antiques store, the expensive children's clothing boutique, the kitchen counter place, and finally round the corner and dart into the marble front entranceway of Haverton Academy.

My head feels enormous—blood is throbbing through my ears and I'm gasping for breath. The air in the hallway feels cool and I step into the strange silence. I am late. Very late. Students are already sorted at desks behind the closed doors, listening to announcements and preparing to take the placement exams. I take a deep breath, and then another one. Sweat trickles down my back, and I can feel it under my armpits, which is *ew*. This is why I am not an athletic person—sooner or later, you are going to have to sweat. I don't like to feel anything oozing from my pores.

Okay. I calm down, stand up straight, and walk forward, trying to move quietly. I'm still hoping that I can slip into class without anyone noticing I was late; I'm still hoping to avoid that last tardy sl—

*Briiiiiiiiiiiiiiiiiing!*

Crap!

*Briiiiiiiiiiiiiiiiiing!*

Why do I have my phone set to the loudest possible setting? I cut it off midring. "Hello?" I whisper.

"Hello? Callie?"

"Cassius! Hi! Did you get my texts?"

"What? No, Callie—I can't read texts, and it's too loud here—"

"Ohmygosh! Oh, Cassius, I'm so sorry, but I have to go to school today it's placement testing and if I miss it—"

"Callie—"

"—if I miss it they'll call my parents and I won't be able to take—"

"Callie—"

"—I won't be able to take any of the electives I want and—"

"Callie." He isn't shouting. If anything, his voice is softer than usual. He sounds small, like he has aged in reverse, or something . . .

"Are you okay?"

"I . . . I'm not sure where I am." He's breathing heavily, and I realize that he's scared.

"What? Wait—where are you?"

"I just said that I don't know!"

"But—where do you think you are? Aren't you at Eighty-Sixth?" That's the subway stop where I was supposed to meet him this morning at eight forty-five.

Where I was supposed to meet him, but didn't.

"I was at Eighty-Sixth, but when you didn't show up, I thought maybe there was a mix-up and you went ahead to the museum without me. I got on the train—but there was some kind of an announcement. I couldn't hear it—"

"Nobody can ever hear those things, it's like someone is trying to speak with a giant tin can on their head! Why don't they—"

"I think I might have gotten on the A or something—"

"Oh my god—"

Sometimes trains run on weird tracks, if there is

construction or a track fire or if someone dies on the train, which happens more often than you would think.

"I got off, but I'm not sure where I am—I can't—it's dark; the signs are so hard to see—" His voice is rising, and I realize that he isn't just scared. He's panicking.

I try to speak in my most soothing voice. "Can you see anything? A sign?"

"There's a mosaic. Tiles—an *M* and an . . . an *H*."

"MH?" That doesn't sound like anything. Why can't he be someplace obvious, like Grand Central? "Okay," I say. "Just breathe . . . Is someone around? Can you ask?"

"I don't want anyone to know that I can't see!"

"Okay."

"There's no one here, anyway—Callie, I think I might be having a heart attack—"

"You're not. You're just freaking out. Trust me, it happens to me all the time. Try to look at a cloud—"

"I'm underground!"

"Breathe! I'll figure it out. I'm coming for you—"

"Callie," he whispers, and then I hear his voice choking. He can hardly speak, and I feel it, I feel it all over my skin that he is weeping. "Callie—I'm going blind."

"I know."

"I'm going blind . . ." He is whispering now.

"I'm coming. I'm coming for you, Cassius." The phone is hot against my cheek, like it might burst into flames. My face is wet, but I don't know if that's from sweat or tears or some other bodily fluid.

"Callie—"

"I'm coming! I'll be right there! Breathe!"

"Thank you—"

I hang up and turn back toward the front door.

But I'm blocked by Ms. Blount.

My history teacher.

## CHAPTER TWENTY-THREE

# In which the heroine reaches for the sky, but ends up in space

"CALLIE VITALIS," Ms. BLOUNT says, eyeing me coolly. "It's so nice to see you."

"Thank you."

"Are you feeling much better?"

"Uh . . ." I fake a cough. "Much better," I say.

"I'm so relieved, as placement testing is this morning. And I do believe that you owe me a revised essay?"

"Right." I pat my bag. "Of course. Got it right here."

Ms. Blount's hair is always sculpted, as if she maybe pours it into a mold and then puts it on her skull. When she tilts her head, her hair stays still, like a hat. It's creepy. "So you had better get to your homeroom."

"I . . . uh . . . I left something . . ."

She checks the gold men's watch that she always wears.

"You have three minutes, Ms. Vitalis."

"Okay . . . right. Thank you." And then I even add, "Good point!" as I back toward the stairs. Once I reach the stairwell, I peek to see if Ms. Blount is going to move on, maybe to terrorize the rest of the hallways. But she doesn't move. She plants herself like a fireplug in front of those double doors.

Poop.

"Pooppooppoop," I whisper. I realize that I can't get out the front door. But there is no way—no way that I'm leaving Cassius on a subway platform. I have to get out of here! I think desperately, looking up the stairs. My classroom is on the fifth floor, and I start trudging up the steps, wondering if I could get out of a window. But I don't want to drop three flights down to the pavement—

And then it hits me—

The fire escape!

You can get to it from the roof! And if there is one place I know how to get to in this whole stupid school, it's the roof!

I run up the stairs, my thighs burning, praying that nobody catches me pleasepleaseplease because I have to get to Cassius. My chest is wheezing and my muscles are aching and I wish that I *were* an exercisey person because then this wouldn't hurt so much and oh my god I just realized I'm going to have to go down seven flights of stairs on a fire escape! But that's too intense to really think about and so I just tell myself *don't look down don't look down don't look down* all the while I am climbing up and up and up . . .

There! I reach for my bag and start searching for the key.

Gah! It's not there! It's supposed to be in the little inside pocket! It must have fallen out. I frantically begin clawing through my bag, which is dumb, because who can find anything in this mess? And finally I think, *Maybe Selena left it unlocked*, so I shove my shoulder against the door, and am shocked when it actually opens. For a moment, I'm blinded by the blue sky, the bright sun, and I close my eyes and suck in a deep breath.

"Callie?"

When I open my eyes, I see Zelda.

CHAPTER TWENTY-FOUR

# In which the heroine realizes that she really doesn't know anything at all

"WHAT—WHAT ARE YOU DOING here?" Zelda asks. She looks frightened and sad and like maybe I caught her doing something that she shouldn't be doing, which is okay, because I am doing the same thing.

"How did you get up here?" I ask her.

"I told Selena that I needed a breath of fresh air. The cleaning lady. She told me that you come up here sometimes."

"That's . . . true. But—listen, the testing is about to start."

"I know." Zelda looks out, over the buildings. Then she peers down at the street below. "We're so far up." Then she looks up at the sky. "And we're so far down."

I look toward the sky, following her glance to where a

white cloud curls overhead, like a dragon tail. "Yes."

"Do you even know what I mean?" The way she asks this is like she doesn't think I possibly could.

"I *do* know what you mean," I say. "Like, we're totally small. And we're totally insignificant—"

"Doesn't it make you feel like nothing you do will ever matter?" The wind lifts her long, blond hair away from her face and it is ridiculous because Zelda seriously looks like she is in a movie right now, but like a *way* different movie from the one I'm in, in which I have to climb down a fire escape and rescue a friend stuck in the subway. "Doesn't it make you feel minuscule?"

"Yeah, but I kind of like that. Like, no matter how much I screw up, it's just—whatever, who cares? We're so *small.*"

"You never screw up, Callie. Your life is perfect."

"WHAT? Ohmygod, WHAT? That is ONE THOUSAND BILLION PERCENT FALSE. How can you even SAY that when you're standing there with your hair streaming out like you're in a Selena Gomez video? YOUR life is perfect. You're beautiful and smart and—"

"Not smart." Zelda swallows and shakes her head. She

looks up at the sky. "Not smart enough."

"Enough for what?" Now my hair is whipping around, and of course it gets stuck in my lip gloss, and I try to spit it out, like *bbbbfffffft,* so I can add, "You're one of the top girls in our class!"

"Not *the* top girl." Zelda looks me in the eye. "Two of my brothers went to Harvard. Even Jimmy went to Dartmouth." Everyone in Zelda's family calls her youngest older brother "Poor Jimmy" because he's not the brightest. "But I'm not even on track to be as good as Jimmy. My scores are—" She shakes her head. "I can't take tests!"

"So what? You can play the cello and take ballet and you're such a good writer, Zelda—"

"Tests, though. That's how you get into good colleges."

"That's, like, FIVE YEARS from now!" My hair is whipping around like crazy, and a piece even gets stuck to my eyeball, but I just wipe it away. Why does it have to be so WINDY? God, I wish I had a KITE right now, but that would be rude considering that my good friend seems to be having a minor nervous breakdown, or whatever.

"No. It's today. If I don't do well on the placements, I won't get into the advanced classes. Janice says that if I'm not in advanced classes in eighth, I won't be in advanced classes for ninth, or tenth—or ever. And then I'll end up going to some third-tier school—"

"Are you crying? Are you crying over a dumb test?!" I just can't even deal with this.

"You don't know what my mother is like!" Zelda's face is twisted and red, and I never thought someone as beautiful as she is could look so hideous. This is a big, fat, messy ugly cry like I must have been doing yesterday (was it just yesterday?) in the Frick with Cassius. And when I think about that, I realize that yesterday, I probably would have thought that Zelda's problem was a big deal, too. And even if it isn't a big deal to me—it's a big deal to her. And I want to help her, but I just can't right now.

I take a deep breath.

"Zelda, we're friends," I tell her. "I want you to know that my life is not perfect. In fact, there's a lot of stuff you don't know about me, okay? Like that my dad lost his job. And we're broke. And I have never met Taylor Swift or been on Beyoncé's yacht. The CW is not making a show based on my cousin's life. I'm not related to the Kardashians. Just—none of it."

"But you look like Khloe!"

"I do *not* look like Khloe; my nose is huge."

Zelda blinks, clearly shocked. "You . . . lied?"

"I lied! About SO. MUCH. STUFF! Taylor Swift never gave me her family's secret recipe for chicken soup! That wasn't even my cousin you met the other day! He's my friend and I have to go and get him because he is going blind and is stuck in the subway and doesn't know where he is."

"Wait—" Zelda twists her fingers through her hair. "Is . . . is *that* true?"

"Yes. That part is true. Now I have to go. But we can talk about your stuff later, okay?"

"You'll miss placement tests!"

"Who cares? I've skipped an entire week of school. I'll probably get kicked out of here, anyway." I stalk over to the edge of the building. The fire escape doesn't come all the way to the roof—just up to the highest window on the floor below—so I carefully lower myself onto it.

"Ohmygod, be careful!" Zelda cries.

I look up at her worried face. It's a strange thing to realize that you totally don't know someone, that underneath the skin you see every day is a whole world that you can't even imagine. And that they can't imagine you, the real you. Not unless you show them. They have no *idea*.

Thoughts like that really make you think.

"Zelda, I've got to go help Cassius." I look up into her worried face. "Would you please tell anyone you see that I was hideously sick, and you put me in a cab home?"

"Yes," she says breathlessly.

I check my phone. "One minute," I tell her, meaning that the test is about to start.

She nods, and turns to go, but a moment later, her head reappears. "Callie," she tells me. "Good luck."

"Same to you," I say. And then I remember what Anna used to always tell me before a test. "Go murder it."

"Okay," she says.

"It's going to be all right. Everything is always changing!" And, as I begin to clatter down the black iron steps of the fire escape, I add, "*Live without regrets!*"

"Okay . . ." Zelda calls after me.

I really hope she can.

## CHAPTER TWENTY-FIVE

# In which I am a SUPERSLEUTH

BY THE TIME I reach the Eighty-Sixth Street subway, I am more sweaty and grimy than I have ever been in my entire life, and a line from a song keeps looping in my mind, singing, "Back of my neck feelin' dirty and gritty/back of my neck feelin' dirty and gritty/back of my neck feelin' dirty and gritty," over and over again until I really just want to shout or make a weird noise to make it go away.

Instead, that stupid song just gets louder as I hustle down the steps and into the subway. Okay, the Studio Museum of Harlem is at 125th Street. At the Eighty-Sixth Street subway stop, you can take the local train, the 6. Or you could go down another level and take the 4 or 5. Which would make more sense, because those are express trains, so they'll make fewer stops before they reach 125th.

That's what Cassius would do, I bet.

I take the steps down again farther. Only a couple of people are down there, which means one of two things:

The train just came and left a minute ago.

Something weird is up with the trains.

So far, I am feeling like Sherlock Holmes, only with better people skills. Flyers are posted on the pilings. The 5 train is, for some mysterious reason, bypassing all station stops until 138th Street—Grand Concourse.

"Grand Concourse?" I say to myself. A middle-aged man in a bomber jacket is standing near me. "Excuse me, can you tell me what neighborhood Grand Concourse is located in?"

"Mott Haven," the guy replies. "Check the map." Then he jerks his thumb toward a map on the wall.

"Mott Haven?" I repeat, but I dimly remember Cassius saying that there were an *M* and an *H* on the wall. I look at the map. Right—the first stop after Eighty-Sixth Street is usually 125th Street. But today it's 138th.

That must be what happened—Cassius got on the 5 and got off at the first stop, but today it's Grand Concourse.

Cassius is in the Bronx.

I wait there for seven minutes (which feels like seven hours, honestly and truly) until a train comes. Finally, it does, and I avoid the totally empty car because I know it must be empty for a good reason—like it's one thousand degrees inside or else someone puked on all the seats—and I get into a nice, clean, not-too-crowded air-conditioned car, and I just sit there while the train clicks and clacks and rumbles on, and zooms me up to Cassius.

When I step out of the train, he is sitting there. He is sitting on one of those strange wooden benches that are left over from 1492, or whenever the subway was first built. He is sitting very straight, staring ahead, looking at the cars but, I know, not really seeing them, at least not well.

"Cassius!" I call out.

I guess I sort of expect him to jump up and run—gazelle-like, and maybe through a field of daisies—over to me and thank me or something, but instead, he closes his eyes and leans his head backward. He just sits there like that as the few strangers from the train pass by, not even noticing this boy who is just staring at the ceiling and . . .

I don't know. Breathing, I guess.

I walk over to him. "Cassius," I say again. And then I sit down beside him.

"You're here," he says, still looking up at the ceiling.

"I'm here. I made it! I totally found you. I was like Nancy Drew—so, like, the 5 was skipping some stops. We're at 138th Street. In the Bronx."

Cassius nods slightly, as if my blathering is still sort of fluttering around his head.

"Isn't it great that I figured out where you were?" I'm a little embarrassed that I felt the need to say this, but I really just kind of want Cassius to be proud of me.

He lifts his head up and looks at me. "What do you think *MH* stands for?" he asks, pointing to a tile mosaic.

"Mott Haven," I tell him, and am a little annoyed that he still hasn't said how, like, impressed he is and how grateful he is, but whatever.

Cassius just nods quickly and takes a little shuddery breath. "I think I'm getting worse," he says. "It's hard to tell, you know, because it's only changing bit by bit when it's happening to you."

"Yeah." Anna got glasses in third grade, and she told

me that she just thought that *everyone* saw a blurry chalkboard. She didn't even realize that her eyesight had gotten worse over the year.

"But it's happening." He sighs. "I can still manage, but . . . Look, I'm sorry I freaked out on you."

"Why are you sorry? Seriously, I don't think you're freaking out *enough*."

Cassius shrugs, and his lips turn down. They look like a steel crowbar. "It's like they say: whatever doesn't kill you makes you stronger."

I stare at him a moment. "Nobody says that."

"Lots of people say it, Callie. They say it to me all the time." He lets out this laugh. It's a bitter laugh. "All the time."

"Anyone who says that to you is a total jerk, because that saying makes zero sense."

He holds out his hands palms-up, like he's going to explain it to me. "Well, emotionally you . . ."

"Are you kidding right now? Going blind is supposed to make you *stronger*? That's—that actually pisses me off." I'm thinking about Grandma Hildy, too. Her son died—did that make her stronger? No! It made her sad.

It made her sad for years. There is a little place in her that will probably be sad for*ever.* The fact is, not everything is something you can get over, okay? I have never heard of this stupid saying before, and I'm glad, because if I saw that written on a mug, I would SMASH THAT MUG!

I think I see something in Cassius's eye—a gleam that might be a tear. But he tips his head backward, and I guess the tears kind of sink back into his eyeballs, because they don't spill out. He breathes for a few minutes, and I breathe, too. I imagine a cloud. It's fat and soft, and lovely. One edge of it curls out, a bit like an arm . . .

"I might need a cane now," Cassius says after a moment.

"Wait! Could you get a dog?"

"It's not like getting a pet dog, Callie." He turns to me and shakes his head. "Don't sound so excited."

"Oh. Will you get to use the handicapped parking spaces?"

"When I drive, you mean?" His voice is sarcastic, and I suddenly realize, *Oh. Of course. Cassius won't drive. Ever.* And, as if he's hearing my thoughts, he adds, "There's just so much."

He doesn't explain, but I know that he means that

there's so much that he'll won't see anymore. The clouds or the ocean. Rainbows. So much art. Or just, faces that make you happy. It makes my chest feel heavy to think about that.

"I think I was maybe having a panic attack," he says.

"It's that kind of day."

Cassius's hands are palms-up on his knees. "Whatever that means."

"Let's go," I say.

"I don't know if I can deal with going home," Cassius says.

"Do you want to just hang out? We could go—we could visit my grandmother and get some cookies, or something."

Cassius nods. Something in the station drips. A man comes down the stairs, walks through the turnstile, and stands at the edge of the platform. Nothing else in the station moves.

"You're a surprisingly cool girl, Callie."

"I know," I say. "And please stop acting like it's so surprising."

But we don't get up right away. Instead, we sit there,

on that stupid wooden bench, with both of our arms on the same armrest, touching. It's an okay subway station, actually, with not too many people and no really noticeable odors.

It's nice to just sit there with Cassius, and while we are sitting there, I forgive him for not thanking me for coming to his rescue and all because I think that it is very important to be able to just sit with someone and not do anything.

That's how you know you're real friends.

## CHAPTER TWENTY-SIX

# In which everything goes bananas

WHEN WE GET OFF of the subway, we head over to Grandma Hildy's apartment, and Robert gives me this weird look in the lobby. But I don't think much of it, and Cassius and I head on up.

I sort of stumble into the apartment, because the sun is shining through the window in a way that nearly blinds me, and I trip over the cat. Cassius bumps into me because I have stopped in my tracks.

"Dad?"

"Who's this?" my father demands, looking at Cassius.

"This is Callie's friend, Cassius," my grandmother says. She is sitting on the wing chair across from the couch, cool as a cucumber. She takes a sip from her yellow coffee mug.

"This is the friend who has been convincing Callie to skip school?" my dad demands.

"Dad! How do you know about that?"

"Did you think we'd never find out?" Dad asks, and his voice is supersarcastic, which just sounds kind of awkward and dumb coming from my dad. "Your school called me. Placement testing is today, but they said you've been out all week?"

"It's not as bad as it—"

"I was *scared*, Callie! I didn't know where you were! I tried to call, but—"

I pull out my phone. Sure enough, there are messages on it. He must have left them when I was in the subway out in the Bronx. And, after that, I wasn't really checking.

"Maybe I should go," Cassius murmurs, but I grab his hand because I cannot be left alone with these people right now.

"When were you going to tell me about school?" Dad demands.

"Um . . ." Hm. That's an interesting question. "Never?"

"Never?" he repeats. "*Never?*"

"Well, of course, you're such a *model* of full

disclosure," my grandmother snaps, and my dad turns to her, but he stops. He stares at the wall. For a moment, he is speechless.

"What happened to the painting of Uncle Larry?" I ask.

Grandma Hildy places her cup on the coffee table, and she doesn't use a coaster, so I know that things are getting serious. "I took it down," she says slowly.

"You took it *down*?" my dad repeats. "Where is it?"

"Hudson, New York."

"*What?*" My dad's face is turning red, and one blue vein looks like it is about to burst out of his forehead.

"Don't get hysterical, George. Callie pointed out to me that I have been seeing it wrong all these years. I thought it was a self-portrait, but it isn't—"

"So what? So you *sold* it? Did it ever occur to you that I might want it?"

"George, I sent the painting to Stephen."

And they stand there like that: Grandma Hildy looking trim in her slacks and kitten heels, and Dad grabbing the back of a chair like he's going to strangle it as the silence falls down around us like snow.

There is a moment when I picture what would happen

if I just ran away, screaming. It seems like an idea with some plausibliciousness. Like, maybe I could get away with it.

But where would I run?

Cassius's hand tightens on mine, and we are having a telepathological moment through our fingers because I know he wants me to say something. The clock on the wall *click, click, clicks*, marking each passing moment, pushing it from the present and into the past and going around, around, around the numbers.

*Not one drop*, Althea Orris says, but these drops have already fallen, and how can I possibly separate them from the ocean now?

These thoughts are *deep.* They're so deep they won't even fit on a tote bag, so deep I can hardly breathe, I can hardly see the light rippling across the surface above me.

"Well, wasn't that a good idea?" I ask finally.

Grandma Hildy's and Dad's eyes are locked on each other, like they are having a wrestling match. "Why would you send the painting to Stephen?" he asks. He sounds as if his mind is working, shifting slowly, like a fog is clearing moment by moment. "Why now?"

"As I was trying to tell you, Callie showed me that it wasn't a self-portrait. It was a painting of Larry looking at Stephen. And I realized that Stephen should have the painting. So I called him." She pauses. "He's lovely."

"I know."

"He was very kind to me, considering."

"He's a kind man."

"Well, I wasn't sure he would want the painting, after all of these years. But he appreciated it very much, and said that he did. He said even though he's married now, that Larry"—Grandma Hildy's eyes drop to her lap—"Larry changed his life."

My dad looks at the blank wall. He just stands there like someone staring into a crystal ball, until finally he takes off his glasses and covers his eyes with his hand. He stands there, making this hissy breathing sound through his nose.

"Is your dad crying?" Cassius whispers. I say, "No," but I think that maybe he is.

Finally, Dad wipes his eyes. He puts his glasses back on. Then he walks over to my grandmother and stands facing her. She looks up at him. I can see her throat working as she swallows, then swallows again.

Cassius says, "I'll go get some water," and hurries to the kitchen. I'm not sure he'll be able to find the glasses, but I don't want to leave my grandmother, who is standing there with tears streaking down her cheeks, creating two streams at once that separate and then rejoin to drip from her jaw, like rain against a window. "I . . . miss . . . my *son*." I look over at Cassius, who has just walked into the room with the "World's Best Grandmother" mug.

"It's all I could find." He sounds like he is apologizing, but my grandmother takes the mug and sips the water.

She places it on her knee, and looks down into the cup, and I wonder if she can see herself reflected there. "I just wish . . . I had been a better mother." Her voice is a whisper and she sounds sick, like all of the crying has made her ill, or maybe it's all the remembering.

"It's not too late, Grandma," I say gently.

Behind me, the clock on the mantel ticks. Grandma Hildy blinks once, and then again. She sways a little, and the whole moment feels like a dream. "You can still be a good mother. You still have a son," I say, pointing to my father. "He's right here."

For a moment, the silence is so profound that I feel like I can hear the daylight crashing through the window.

And then everyone is like WOW, CALLIE, you are SO DEEP, and we all gather around for this totally magical group hug, and sparks and a rainbow float through the room and Cyndi Lauper appears from behind the couch to sing *True Colors* and it's this enchanted moment that I know I'll remember all my life.

Well, actually, not that.

What happens is that my grandmother stares at my dad like he's someone she maybe only vaguely recognizes. The clock ticks on.

"Why did I listen to him?" my grandmother whispers. "I couldn't argue with Constantine. I never could."

"I know, Mom." My dad wipes a tear from her cheek.

"I thought there would be more time . . ."

"I think Larry did, too," my father says gently. "It happened really quickly, at the end."

My grandmother's eyes are bright. Isn't it strange how tears can look like glass, or even diamonds? "He can never forgive me . . ." Grandma Hildy takes a shuddering breath.

My father doesn't say anything, because what could he say? Time only travels in one direction. Each second we're alive carries us further from the past. We can visit in our dreams and memories, but we can't stay there. Even Mr. Johnson has to leave apartment 1986 to get his coffee.

My mother says that we have to live without regrets, but I don't think that's possible. The trick, I think, is to learn to live *with* them, because regrets are the moments in life that teach us the most. You can't change the past, but you can try to learn from it. That's not the kind of thought that looks good on a coffee mug, but it's true.

"If I could do it over, I'd do things differently," Grandma Hildy says.

Cassius clears his throat. "Muhammad Ali said, 'A man who sees the world the same way at fifty as he did at twenty has wasted thirty years of his life,'" he says.

Grandma Hildy nods slowly. "Thank you, Cassius." And I think about how I should go home and read some books by Muhammad Ali because he is truly an amazing philosopher.

Finally, my dad says, "You did the right thing, Mom. Sending the painting to Stephen. I'm glad you did."

Her delicate eyebrows lift in surprise. "Thank you, George."

He leans down and gives her a hug. She squeezes back,

and this is officially the first time that I have seen them do that. It looks kind of awkward, but I think they will get better, with practice. Finally, my dad straightens up. "Come on, Callie. It's time to go."

My grandmother looks at me, and when she reaches out, I give her hand a squeeze. I am proud that she sent Uncle Larry's painting to Stephen, and I am remembering this thought I had a few days ago, that a journey of a thousand miles begins with a single step, but it also ends with one. I think that actually does make sense, after all. "Everything's going to be okay," I say, and I really mean it.

Dad places a hand on my grandmother's shoulder. "Try to rest, Mom," he says.

I give her a good-bye kiss, and then I follow Dad out the door. I kind of forgot about Cassius, but he trails after us.

We stand in silence while we wait for the elevator. When it comes, we get in. We are silent for almost the entire trip down, but somewhere around the seventh floor, my dad asks, "Are you named after Muhammad Ali, by any chance?"

"Dad, his name is *Cassius*," I say just as Cassius says, "Yes."

And I think, *That does not make any sense*, but really nothing does today, so I just leave it alone.

"I'll be very interested to hear what you and Callie have been up to," my dad says, and when I start to speak, my father says, "You can tell me at home, Callie."

"Okay," I say. And I think that he really will be interested when I tell him the story. I think he might even like the educational museum-y parts. Because here is one thing I have learned this week: *life is way more educational than school.* Muhammad Ali even said so.

Anyone who doesn't agree probably just hasn't done enough living yet.

## CHAPTER TWENTY-SEVEN

# In which: soup

WE HAVE JUST STEPPED out of the lobby of my grandmother's apartment building and started toward Madison Avenue when someone shouts, "Ohmygosh, Callie!"

Min is running up behind us, holding up a paper bag with one hand and waving with the other. "Callie! Are you okay? I was coming over to your place!" She stops and smiles at my dad. "Hi, Mr. Vitalis. I'm so glad you're better. I made you guys more of that Taylor Swift soup!"

"When did you make it?" I ask. "School just got out."

"I made it last night and brought it to Haverton! I thought you could have it for lunch."

Cassius is looking at me with his nostrils, as always.

His look says, *Are you going to trust this friend?*

I shoot a glance at my dad, and say, "Um, Min—I—I wasn't sick today."

"I know."

"And Taylor Swift didn't give me that recipe."

"Yeah."

"Did Zelda tell you?"

"Yeah, but I wasn't really surprised."

"You—?"

"Callie—" my dad prompts.

"Dad, could I have just—just *five* minutes?"

He nods, and I turn back to my friend. My head is swirling, and I'm not really sure what to say.

"Why did you lie?" Min asks.

"I just—" I don't really know the answer to this. "The truth just seemed . . . too . . ." My voice trails off, like steam rising into the air.

Min looks over at Cassius. "Is this your cousin?"

"Hi! I'm from Cleveland, Nevada," Cassius says, and my dad is all, "What?"

"Min, no—this is my friend, Cassius."

"The one in the subway?" She points surreptitiously

to her eyes, and I nod. "Nice to meet you." Then she turns back to me. "Look, we'll find someone to buy your ticket. Don't worry. Lots of people like Lucas Zev."

"You got tickets to the *Lucas Zev* concert?" Cassius says. "Wow."

"Do you want to come? The ticket's expensive—two hundred and fifty—but we're in the first row."

"I'm there," Cassius says. "Definitely."

"See?" Min turns to me with a brilliant smile. "Problem solved!"

I open my mouth to speak. Fail. Finally, I sputter, "You don't even know Cassius!"

"He's your friend, isn't he?" Min says. "It's not a big deal, Callie. It's all fixed now." She takes a deep breath. "Zelda's kind of mad, but she'll get over it."

"Will she?"

"It's not like Zelda always tells the truth, you know? I mean, we all have secrets, right?" Min's eyes lock on mine.

"Yeah," I say at last. "I guess . . . I guess everyone does." And I wonder what Min's secret is, and if we will ever be good enough friends for her to tell me.

Min nods, then hands me the bag. "Take the soup," she

says. "You'll need it. You have to tell your mom everything?"

"Yeah . . ." I think this over a moment. "But—you know what? I don't think it'll be that bad. In this weird way, I'm actually kind of looking forward to it." I look her in the eye and smile. "It's good to tell the truth. Live without regrets."

"That's what my mom always says."

"Really? Mine, too!"

Min smiles, and I think that right there, right in that moment, we came one millimeter closer to being real friends. "And you—" She turns to Cassius. "Can Callie text me your info? We can pick you up at seven."

"Great. Call me, though. I'm not so great with texts."

"Sure." Then Min gives me a little kiss on the cheek. "Bye, Mr. Vitalis."

"Good-bye, Min. Thanks for the soup."

It's funny—I never really considered Min my friend. I mean, she's my texting friend, and my nice friend, but not, like, a *good* friend. I always thought she was kind of shallow. And maybe a little . . . um, dumb. Like my history teacher thought *I* was dumb, I guess.

But Cassius is right. You can't really know what someone is like until you trust them enough to show them what *you're* like. And sometimes they let you down.

But sometimes they *don't*.

And those are the times that you find out who someone really is. And you might even get some soup out of it.

## CHAPTER TWENTY-EIGHT

## In which my dad comes clean

My father puts Cassius in a cab and gives the driver a twenty-dollar bill, even though Cassius insists that he is fine and could easily walk home.

"This is the least I can do," my dad assures him. "You know all of our family secrets now."

"That's okay." Cassius's fingers hang over the edge of the window. "Callie knows all of mine. Hey—Studio Museum tomorrow? It's Saturday."

"If I'm not grounded," I tell him.

"She'll be grounded," my dad says. "But maybe you guys can meet after school one day."

"Sounds good. Maybe it'll be Callie's one and only extracurricular!" Cassius's laugh trails after the cab pulls away, and my father and I begin walking downtown, toward home.

Up the block is the Metropolitan Museum. It's enormous. *That could easily be an extracurricular*, I think. *I'd happily go there every week, with Cassius.*

My father's voice drifts over to me. "Why didn't you tell us that you were failing history?"

It takes me a moment to understand the question. Finally, I say, "Ms. Blount thinks I plagiarized a paper, but I didn't. She thinks I'm too dumb to write a good essay on ancient Egyptian funerary practices. She said if I 'wrote my own paper' by the end of the week, she wouldn't call you and Mom."

"You didn't plagiarize it?"

"No! I worked on it for *weeks*. I spent every weekend in the Egyptian collection, remember?"

"And something about detentions? And skipping school?"

"I just—I needed to be alone. Sometimes, I get stressed out. And lonely, I guess. It isn't easy, being at a new school . . ."

"I didn't realize you felt that way."

"Well, I would sometimes just go up to the roof. Just to breathe. But that made me late to class a few times. So if

I was late once more, they were going to call you. So then I was running late one morning, and it was just easier to skip school and text in an excuse than deal with another tardy. And then it kind of . . . got a little out of control."

"Why didn't you let them call us?"

"Because you guys are crazy right now." My dad makes a little noise, and I realize how bad that sounds. "Busy," I add quickly. "Crazy-busy."

"No . . ." Dad's voice is slow. "I think . . . crazy. I didn't know you were picking up on all of it."

"It's a little hard to miss," I tell him. We are on the side of the street by the park, and we pass a bench with a woman and a baby in a stroller, then another with a man surrounded by large plastic bags filled with empty bottles. Then there is a free bench, and my dad walks over to it. We both sit down.

I look up and try to focus on the wisp of cloud I see, because I have a terrible, sick feeling that my father and I are going to have a Serious Talk, and if there is anything on earth that is worse than that, I don't know what it is.

"Callie, there are a few things you should know. When I took the job at the fund, I thought it was legitimate. But

I quickly discovered that there were . . . inconsistencies in the accounting."

"That's why it went bankrupt," I say, but my dad keeps on going.

"I reported everything to my bosses, but I was told that this was their accounting and, well, basically, I was told to shut up."

"But you didn't shut up."

"Well . . . no. I *did* shut up. For a little while. But the market started to take a dive, and—it's kind of complicated. I started to worry about the people who had invested with us. I just—I had to report it. So I did."

"You called the cops?"

"I contacted the SEC. The money cops. It turned out that the fund was already under investigation, so I cooperated. But, look—there are two points I wanted to make. The first point is that things might be rough for a while. I might have to pay some money to the lawyer, and the fund isn't paying me anymore, so we might have to sell the apartment, or work something out. I don't know."

"Okay," I say, although it is not exactly okay. But now I see why my mom has been so stressed out. And what she meant when she said that he always does what he thinks is right, even when it's hard.

"The second thing I wanted to tell you is that I only regret one thing about this whole mess—I regret not reporting the fund sooner. I knew it was wrong, and I let it go on, and there might be some people who are going to lose their money because of me." He turns and looks at me.

"But you fixed it."

"As well as I could. Not everything can *be* fixed."

"No . . ." I know that we are both thinking about Grandma Hildy. But I am also thinking about Cassius, and his eyesight. These things that can't be fixed. "They can be softened, though," I say, and I know that this did not come out right, but what I mean is that it helps to have people who understand.

"Callie, next time, please don't wait to tell us if you're in trouble. We're your parents. We may not be perfect, but we love you." My dad picks up my hand, and when we lace our fingers together, I'm surprised that mine are almost as long as his now.

"Dad . . . I feel the same way. I mean, I love you. You can tell me stuff."

My dad looks surprised for a moment. Then he nods. "Okay, Callie."

"And I think you should listen to Desmond, too."

Dad winces. "I didn't do the right thing with the lunch bag."

"Neither did I. Neither did anyone. Except—well, except for Desmond."

"Except for Desmond."

We both think about that for a while.

"Are you going to—can you forgive Grandma Hildy?"

"Forgive her? I don't have to forgive your grandmother. I'm not mad at—"

"Then how come she's not ever allowed to give me or Desmond money? How come you never visit her, unless you get a call from the school? How come you didn't tell her about the fund?"

Dad looks at the cobblestones. "I—" But he can't finish the thought, and throws up his hands. Then he folds them across his chest. "Maybe I *do* need to forgive her."

"I don't know."

Then he holds my hand again. "We've got a lot of stuff to tell your mother."

"Hm," I say. "Let's make sure she has a glass of wine first."

We sit there for a long time, holding hands, and having a moment as well as anyone can have a moment in New York City. A squirrel scampers past us with half a giant bagel in its mouth, and a bald guy wearing a business suit and a crown of flowers hails a taxi, and a tiny blond woman pumping small dumbbells power-walks by, followed by her muscle-bound trainer in a T-shirt that reads "BEAST," and I feel like my dad and I are an island at the center of the stormy ocean. In the immortal words of Cyndi Lauper, the calm inside the storm is something only life can bring.

That, actually, would make a good mug.

"Wouldn't it be funny if Grandma married Mr. Johnson, and she moved into his apartment, and then we moved into *her* apartment?" I say suddenly.

My dad's eyebrows rise up toward his hairline. "That . . . is not very likely."

"It *could* happen, though," I say. "I mean, if they ever start dating. And if we have to sell our apartment anyway."

"It could happen," my dad admits.

I think about maybe concentrating on this idea a little,

and maybe trying to Althea-Orris it into happening. But then I decide to forget it. That whole positive-thought thing hasn't really helped at all. In fact, it has kind of only made things worse. And sometimes bad things just happen—bad thoughts have nothing to do with it. Look at Cassius. Look at Uncle Larry and Grandma Hildy. Look at Desmond. Look at *everyone in the world.*

"I can hope, though," I say aloud. "I can dream."

"You?" My dad smiles at me. "I don't think you can stop."

I look up again, trying to catch sight of the wisp of cloud I saw earlier, but it's gone. I can still see other clouds passing across the sky, up there beyond the new leaves. One of the amazing things about the sky is that it's always worth looking at. You never look at the same sky twice, you know what I mean?

So that, I guess, is what I would say to people, if I had an official philosophy: don't forget to look at the sky, because it's still there, even when you are stuck in the subway.

Okay, that's kind of deep, but still not perfect.

I'm working on it.

# Acknowledgments

Whenever I teach a workshop or give a lecture, someone asks where I get my ideas. Here is the thing about ideas: they pop up all of the time, absolutely everywhere. But, unfortunately, not all of those ideas are good.

The problem is that I can't always tell if an idea is bad. Sometimes, I don't know if it's a dead end, or if something that looks like a bad idea actually has a story lurking inside, or if a bunch of lousy little ideas have sneaked their way into my mostly good-idea novel and mucked it up. For that, I have to rely on my friends and colleagues. I am very lucky to be surrounded with people who are much more talented than I am—people who have a gift for honestly (yet kindly) assessing the good and the bad in a novel.

When I came up with the idea for *Apartment 1986*, I

didn't have much faith in it. But when I described it to my longtime friend and former editor, Helen Bernstein, she put her hand over her heart at the ending. "Write that one," she said. "Write that next." So I wrote a bit of it, but I wasn't sure if it was funny. I sent a few pages to Ellen Wittlinger, a fantastic writer with whom I have been in a critique group for the past ten years. She wrote, "Lisa, it's hilarious! You must write this." So I kept going. The next step was a working retreat at the Writing Barn in Austin, Texas, where author Nicole Griffin gave me feedback on the first fifty pages and helped me hammer out my plans for the rest of the story. Once I had a finished first draft, the manuscript went to my critique group, where Ellen, Liza Ketchum, Pat Collins, and Nancy Werlin offered their incredibly helpful input. Another two months of work, and it was time for my agent and editor to look at it. Rosemary Stimola and Kristen Pettit offered their invaluable insight and support, and I got back to work. I sent a copy of the almost-finished manuscript to Johanna Silva, who read it in three days and gave me feedback and information on life for someone with limited vision. Two more rounds of revisions from Kristen and . . . finally . . . I had a novel.

As Callie would say, it takes a village to write a book.

So I would like to thank all of these people for the hard work and care they put into assessing my work, their honesty, and—most of all—their encouragement. I could never have written this book without you, mostly because I wouldn't have wanted to. You all are the part of writing that I like best.

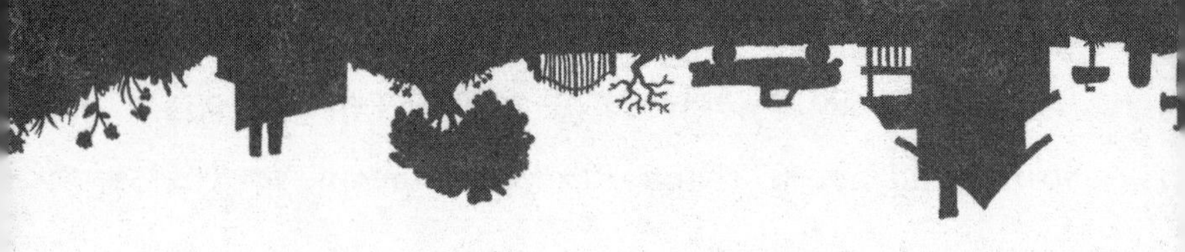

Read on for a peek at Lisa Papademetriou's
*A Tale of Highly Unusual Magic!*

NOBODY HAD EVER TOLD Kai that she should hold her breath when passing by a graveyard, but she did it anyway. She held it and gripped the door handle of the massive powder blue 1987 Dodge pickup as her great-aunt barreled bat-crazy past a large iron gate and up the driveway. Kai gaped through the smudgy truck window at ancient crosses and crumbling white grave markers that hunched, lurking, behind the sagging iron gate. "You live by a graveyard?" she asked, squeezing the door handle like she might just jump out.

"Quiet neighbors!" Great-Aunt Lavinia yelled so Kai could hear her over the Jay-Z song blaring through the radio. The Big Ol' Truck spat gravel as Lavinia slammed the brakes, lurching to a stop. She leaned against the steering wheel and turned to face Kai. "And they never complain about my music." Lavinia cranked up the volume for a moment, rapping along, then switched it off with a wink. "Most people round here like country, but I can't stand it."

"Okay," Kai said, because she thought she should say something. Conversation wasn't really her strongest subject, to tell you the truth.

"You like country?"

"Uh, no."

"Well, all right, because you ain't gonna hear much of it in my house." Lavinia yanked open the door and spilled out. With a deft move, she put one foot on top of the rear tire and hauled herself over the edge of the cargo bed, grabbing Kai's bag and violin case.

Kai wasn't nearly as swift—or as smooth. Gingerly, she pulled back the handle and looked down at the gravel driveway. It seemed like it was about forty feet below her.

"Do you need me to come and get you, sugar?" Lavinia called from the front steps.

"Coming." Clinging to the door, Kai managed to awkwardly half swing, half sprawl onto the pavement. She dusted off her hands and slammed the truck door, giving it a pat as she hurried toward the house.

And what a house!

It had a high peaked roof, and a front porch that had been nearly swallowed up by creeping vines and aggressive shrubbery. A bush with flowers big enough to sit in bloomed just beyond the vines' reach. Everything seemed to join together at odd, tilted angles, as if the house had come home late and rumpled from a particularly wild House Party. A tired picket fence lined the property, and a crooked gate complained at every breeze. The whole place looked like it belonged in a book, but perhaps one that wasn't very nice. I'm talking one where the children get gobbled up in the end.

A mailbox crouched at the end of the footpath. A name was painted on the sign in elegant silver letters. *Quirk*, it read.

*You got that right*, Kai thought.

So far, her great-aunt Lavinia was a bit . . . odd.

"Your father always called her Auntie Lavinia, but she's actually your great-great-grandfather's cousin, so she must be eighty or ninety years old by now," Kai's mother, Schuyler, had said right before putting Kai on a plane. "She probably needs a lot of help around the house, the poor, frail old thing. You'll try to be helpful, won't you?"

Let me tell you that Great-Aunt Lavinia was about as frail as a Sherman tank. Kai was never good at judging heights, but I am, and I can tell you that Lavinia was over six feet tall. She carried Kai's suitcase like it was a pocketbook. Kai guessed that she was sixty, but this was one thing that Kai's mother had right: Lavinia would turn eighty-seven at the end of the summer. She had a few wrinkles at the corners of her mouth and eyes, and she had gray hair. But the gray hair was long, almost down to her waist, and held back in a thick braid. Lavinia wore jeans. Not the grandma kind, either, but dark-wash skinny jeans, and red Converse sneakers. Her fingers were full of chunky turquoise jewelry. She looked hip and fashionable, despite the fact that she was shaped a bit like a turnip and one of her eyes was bigger than the other.

*This lady,* Kai thought as she trotted after her great-aunt, *does* not *need my help around the house.*

Kai hesitated in the doorway a moment, but Lavinia was already jogging up the wide wooden staircase, calling, "Your room is up here, sweets!"

Kai followed, but she didn't hurry. She ran her hand along the dark banister. It was the kind she had always wished for—perfect for sliding down. Back home, Kai lived in a square gray apartment building with an unreliable elevator.

At the top of the landing, Kai found a long hallway. "This one here is the guest room." Lavinia's voice floated to her from a room on the right. Kai followed the sound and stepped into a lovely white room with a dark wood four-poster bed and matching bureau. An old, smoky mirror reflected gentle light, and crammed bookshelves lined an entire wall. An overstuffed chair lounged in the corner near a window seat that overlooked the front lawn. At home, Kai slept on a mattress on the floor, and shoved her clothes into oversize plastic storage boxes. Her mother didn't believe in spending money on furniture—every spare penny went to Kai's college fund. To Kai, this seemed like a room from a magazine, or a pleasant dream.

"Pretty," Kai said.

"Ain't it?" Lavinia put the suitcase down by the bed and turned to face Kai. "So, listen. I don't know how to say this, so I'm just gonna come out and say it. I can't help it if it hurts your feelings." Lavinia's fingertips dipped into the smallest pocket of her jeans. "I don't know what to do with kids."

"Me, either."

Lavinia cocked her head, as if she couldn't tell whether or not Kai was teasing her. She wasn't. Kai really didn't get most kids. They didn't get her, either.

"All right, sugar." Lavinia gave Kai a pat on the arm. "I'm just going to do . . . what I do. I'm not going to entertain you."

"Fine. Great, actually."

Lavinia stood perfectly still for a moment. So did Kai.

Around them, the house was enormous and silent. "Okay, then," Lavinia said at last. "There's food in the fridge. I don't keep any soda or junk, though. If you want that stuff, you can go walk to the Walgreens."

"By myself?"

"Why not? You're twelve, ain't ya? I was walkin' to the store by myself at age five."

The thought of walking around in a strange town all alone made Kai feel fizzy, like a can of soda that's been shaken up. "Can I poke around the house?"

"Suit yourself." Lavinia fussed with a curtain for a moment, and then she walked out of the room.

Kai stood beside the window for a moment, just smelling the air in the room. It smelled like clean, old things. She walked over and scanned the books on the shelves. A leather-bound book with gold lettering on the spine caught her eye. *The Exquisite Corpse,* it said. Kai pulled it out. She didn't mind creepy titles. She kind of liked them, in fact.

*Greetings, salutations, and welcome to the Exquisite Corpse!* It began. *Just as your grandmother and grandfather used to play the old parlor game in which one person would draw a head, and then fold it over, and another would draw a body, and another would draw legs, and so on—you will breathe life into a creature of your own making. You are about to embark on a journey of magic beyond your powers of discernment, imagination, and belief! All it takes is one person bold enough to set the story in motion!*

*Let the magic begin!*

Beneath this, someone with excellent handwriting had written the name Ralph T. Flabbergast.

There was something about the book that made her shaken-up feeling come back again. And then Kai did something that she never really understood. She pulled a pen from her pocket. After *Ralph T. Flabbergast*, she wrote, *was a complete fool.*

She looked down at the page, dread pricking across her skin on little insect feet. *I shouldn't have done that,* she thought. *That was rude.* Not that Ralph was likely to care. He'd been dead for almost fifty years.

Outside, the sun shone bright and high. She had been

sitting in an airplane for almost four hours, which made her restless. There was no reason to stay indoors. Kai decided to go explore the neighborhood.

It was her second mistake.